Misfits and Miracles

Also available in the Road to Avonlea Series

Next in the Series...

Misfits and Miracles

Storybook written by

Linda Zwicker

Based on the Sullivan Films Production
written by Heather Conkie
adapted from the novels of

Lucy Maud Montgomery

HarperCollins*Publishers*Ltd

MISFITS AND MIRACLES
Storybook written by Linda Zwicker

Copyright © 1992 by HarperCollins Publishers Ltd,
Sullivan Films Distribution Inc., and
Ruth Macdonald and David Macdonald

Based on the Sullivan Films Production produced by Sullivan Films Inc.
in association with CBC and the Disney Channel with the participation of Tele-
film Canada adapted from Lucy Maud Montgomery's novels.

Road to Avonlea is the trademark of Sullivan Films Inc.

Teleplay written by Heather Conkie
Copyright © 1990 by Sullivan Films Distribution Inc.

Canadian Cataloguing in Publication Data
Zwicker, Linda
Misfits and miracles
(Road to Avonlea ; 20)
Based on the Sullivan Films Production adapted from the novels of
Lucy Maud Montgomery
ISBN 0-00-647390-3

I. Title. II. Series.

PS8599.W53M57 1992   jC813'.54   C92-094625-9
PZ7.Z95M57 1992

Design by Andrew Smith Graphics Inc.
92 93 94 95 96 ❖ OFF 10 9 8 7 6 5 4 3 2 1

Chapter One

A crisp, cracking noise startled Sara awake. It was like a rifle shot! Then there was another one! Sara tugged the comforter snug to her chin, too afraid and too cold to get out of bed. She didn't know what time it was, but the sun was shining brightly and she could hear Aunt Olivia and Aunt Hetty moving around in the kitchen downstairs.

There was a soft knock at Sara's door as she lay in bed, trying to summon the courage to settle her feet on the frigid floor. Her bedroom, to put it bluntly, was freezing.

"Sara? Are you awake?" Aunt Olivia sounded shivery.

"I'm not sure!" called Sara, stalling for time.

Aunt Olivia opened the door and popped her head around. She hugged her shawl close. "You'd better get up, Sara, we've got a problem."

Sara's eyes widened. "The gunshot, Aunt Olivia?"

Olivia looked distracted. "Gunshot? Oh, no, that wasn't a gunshot, Sara. It's just that sometimes when it gets this cold, the trees crack horrifically."

"That's amazing!" said Sara, as she scrambled out of bed. "So what's the problem?" Sara loved problems. Problems could turn into disasters, and disasters could turn into adventures, and adventures were always interesting. "Or is it a disaster?" Sara asked dramatically.

Olivia chewed on her lip—a habit of hers when she was upset.

"The chimney seems to be blocked. We can't light the stove in the kitchen. And I'm afraid to use the fireplace in the parlor. It's been smoking so badly, and that just makes the parlor sooty."

Sara looked encouraging.

Olivia pressed on. "And Hetty is feeling quite dreadful. You know how she always overdoes it at Christmas! Now she's running a fever, and Muriel Stacey is arriving tomorrow and there's baking to be done and it's the coldest day of the winter so far and—oh, dear, Sara—maybe it *is* a disaster!" She plunked down on Sara's bed, looking quite frazzled.

"How can I help, Aunt Olivia?" asked Sara, earnestly.

Hetty groped for a fresh handkerchief in the deep pockets of her heavy wool skirt and sneezed for the fifth time in a row. Now, there are a wide variety of sneezes. There are discreet little snorts, generous blasts, and then there are the "build-up" sneezes—the ones that rise and rise in an astonishing crescendo and finish with a mighty roar. Unfortunately, Hetty's sneezes fell into the "mighty roar" category.

"Now Sarah, I want—want—want—" Hetty gripped the side of the table. Sarah's cat, Topsy, sped from the kitchen. Sara and Olivia leaned back. Another sneeze thundered forth. Poor Hetty! She really did look frightful, with her blotchy face buried in her handkerchief.

"God bless, Hetty," intoned Olivia.

"God bless," echoed Sara.

"I need more than God's blessings today, thank you very much" snapped Hetty. "I need a working stove, a warm house and the strength to get me through Muriel Stacey's visit!" She blew her nose defiantly.

Ever since Muriel Stacey had written confirming her visit to Avonlea in the new year, Hetty had been in a state. A controlled state, mind you, but she had been noticeably sharper than usual both at school and at home. This was understandable, thought Sara, because, after all, Miss Stacey had been appointed Provincial Superintendent of Schools, when Hetty had hoped for the honor. However, Sarah thought Miss Stacey's previous visit had laid that matter to rest. There must be something else bothering Aunt Hetty—something more than the fact that Muriel Stacey would be staying at Rose Cottage—something Sara couldn't put her finger on. Well, nothing ventured, nothing gained.

"Aunt Hetty, why don't you like Miss Stacey?"

Hetty bristled. "Whatever are you talking about, Sara? Olivia, don't put so much butter on that bread! We're a bit short on butter as it is. Heaven knows where it gets to."

Olivia spoke quietly. "Hetty, I am doing the best I can to prepare breakfast without any fire for making porridge or toast. I know you're feeling wretched, but I really don't appreciate you shouting at me."

The two sisters regarded each other across the chilly kitchen. Aunt Hetty sniffed sharply.

"Oh, you poor dear," clucked Olivia, as she passed Hetty a clean handkerchief. Hetty nodded her thanks and the little tiff was over.

Sara bit into a piece of bread and butter generously smeared with strawberry jam. It would be so nice, she thought, to have a sister. Someone you could really talk to and share secrets with, and maybe even write stories about. Of course, her cousin Felicity was very dear to Sara, but she didn't have that deep, poetic soul that Sara was sure a real sister would have. Sara sighed.

"Sara! Sara, are you listening to me?" Aunt Hetty looked flushed, even though the house was cold.

"Yes, Aunt Hetty."

"I want you to stay here with Aunt Olivia while I walk to Pat Frewen's for help. There's no point my going to Alec and Janet's. Alec is off to Markdale today to pick up wood, and we must get this chimney cleared, and quick about it."

"But Aunt Hetty," cried Sara, "you can't! You're sick and you might—well, you just can't, can she, Aunt Olivia?"

Olivia spoke firmly. "Sara's quite right, Hetty. It's entirely out of the question. It would be foolish to risk your health in such a fashion. I'll go."

"No!" yelped Sara, so loudly that both her aunts snapped to attention. "I can run the fastest, and I'll get to Mr. Frewen's farm in a flash."

Hetty looked unconvinced. "Sara, I really think you're too young to —"

"Aunt Hetty, please, I'm twelve years old and the storm's past and it's only snow and I know my way backwards!"

"But do you know it forwards?" teased Olivia.

"Please?" begged Sara. She wanted to be out, doing something useful.

Hetty paused and blew her nose again. She hated to be ill, seeing it as a defect of character rather than an unbidden event. But ill she was. Reluctantly, she nodded her permission.

Sara popped up from the table and sprinted towards the hallway.

"Sara!" croaked Hetty. "Horses gallop. Young ladies walk." But Sara was already halfway up the stairs to her bedroom.

Hetty raised her voice hoarsely to reach her.

"Mind you put on your warmest leggings now, and an extra undershirt and—and—" Another violent sneeze ended Hetty's instructions in an abrupt fashion.

As Sara walked towards Pat Frewen's farm, in the sparkling white world Avonlea had become, memories of Christmas, now a few days past, began rolling around in her mind, like marbles in a pocket. She let them spin as she crunched along in the glistening snow.

Christmas Day, the entire King clan had gathered at Rose Cottage for a merry dinner. Since Hetty was the eldest King, and very dedicated to carrying on family traditions, she had exhausted herself with days of preparation. There was a magnificent feast—a monumental goose, savory roast potatoes, creamed onions, an amazing variety of jellied salads and, to top it off, a blazing carrot-and-rum pudding. And that wasn't all! As the evening progressed and everyone joined in singing carols and playing Chinese Checkers, Janet produced two large tins of her famous maple walnut fudge, a tin of melt-in-your-mouth shortbread and a chocolate ripple cake! Sara ate too much. Everyone ate too much. But, as Uncle Alec proclaimed, "It's only once a year." Aunt Janet was very pleased, and so was thirteen-year-old Felicity, Sara's older cousin, who had undertaken the fudge preparations for the first time.

Increasingly, Felicity was taking on the responsibilities of the King household. This was because Janet was very pregnant. The baby was due any day now, or at least that's what Dr. Blair reported. And, without being unkind, Janet King was extremely large. She never was a small woman, but now, as the next King was about to arrive on the scene, her size was the object of great curiosity among Sara and her three King cousins. They talked about "what was in there" and about whether Felicity, Felix and Cecily would have a little brother or a little sister—or even twins!

The children had even speculated about how babies were born, but Felix, with all the assurance of an eleven-year-old, had made a horrible face and said it was disgusting, and everyone had agreed and started to play a boisterous game of tag. Still, as Sara had observed Janet, sitting large and flushed in the big chair in the parlor on Christmas Day, she'd wondered about the momentous process of birth, and how it all happened.

Boxing Day a terrific wind had arisen, sweeping up enormous waves that roared and snarled against the sand shore. This had lasted for two days, and the people who struggled into town to pick up mail or get a few groceries could hardly share a greeting on the street before the words were whipped out of their mouths and sent whirling down the road. The temperature plummeted. All of Avonlea, all of Prince Edward Island, was caught in the vise of icy winter weather.

"It's colder than a moose at midnight!" declared Pat Frewen, cheerfully. Although no one was quite sure what this meant, everyone agreed that Avonlea's finest pig farmer had coined a colorful description.

Then yesterday, New Year's Day, it had snowed—and snowed. It was impossible to go anywhere, so domestic amusements were the order of the day. But

Sara had felt strangely out-of-sorts, considering that it was the most festive time of year. For one thing, she felt fat. This wasn't surprising, since she'd enjoyed all the holiday feasting but hadn't been able to stick her nose outdoors for a little exeercise. But her mood was more than the result of indigestion. There was an aching restlessness in Sara's soul.

Christmas Day, when she'd been searching for her best blue taffeta sash, she'd stumbled upon a doll in her clothes closet. The doll had been sent by Sara's father last year from Paris, as a Christmas gift. It was exquisite. A halo of honey-golden hair framed her delicate porcelain face, and a pale-mauve silk dress graced her perfect body. She even had a little engraved silver locket around her graceful neck. The elegant script on the locket announced her name—Mimi. But she was too beautiful to play with, thought Sara. Untouchable, like Sarah's father. So Mimi lay on a shelf in Sara's clothes closet, mute and still.

The truth was that, although Christmas had been happy and busy, Sara, in her deepest heart, missed her father and mother terribly. Now her father was gone too—killed in an accident at his warehouse. Even though she was surrounded by people who loved her, Sarah felt alone, an orphan. She didn't say anything out loud about this, and in fact tried to push the sorrow away. Aunt Hetty and Aunt Olivia were very kind, but the sad fact was that they couldn't replace Sara's real parents.

Eventually, the memories had become too painful, and Sara had curled up on the horsehair sofa and tried to distract herself by reading a handsome illustrated book Aunt Hetty had given her for Christmas called *Delightful Stories of Persons and Things*. From time to time she'd looked out the front window and watched as the world disappeared into a white, howling, whirling mass. Snow grew on the fenceposts, the veranda railings, the front steps of Rose Cottage. Topsy ventured out into the whiteness, lifted his paws in alarm and streaked back into the warmth of the parlor. It had been a day for reading and drinking tea. It had been a day for recovering from the hurly-burly of the holidays.

Well, memories were all very well, thought Sara, as she clumped along in the fresh snow towards Pat Frewen's farm, but there were chimneys to be cleared and stoves to be lit, and Hetty and Olivia were counting on her. Sara gazed up at the trees flanking the road, struck by the beauty of the sun as it danced on the crystal branches, dazzling and confident. It suddenly occurred to Sara that she had been walking for quite a while. In fact, Sara realized that, by now, she should have turned into the lane leading to Pat Frewen's farm. She stopped, confused. She turned around. She couldn't see Rose Cottage. She couldn't see Pat Frewen's farm. She couldn't see anything she recognized! The deep snowfall had transformed the familiar landscape into soft, alien shapes, mounded and menacing. Sara's heart hammered. In a swift and terrifying flash, she knew she was lost.

Chapter Two

"TIMBER!" bellowed Archie Gillis as a towering spruce tree started to crack and splinter its way to the frosty ground. Jeb Ryan and Zeke Sloane grabbed their axes and jumped clear of the tree as it thundered heavily earthward, just missing Peg Bowen's cabin. Archie's hefty son, thirteen-year-old Rupert, stood close by, cheering as birds screamed and flew up, their home giving way beneath them. Then, once the spruce had rocked and finally settled on the forest floor, there was silence.

"Good work, men!" shouted Archie. "Jeb, bring up that team of horses. Zeke, get to work hacking off the branches so we can haul this off. Rupert and I will go up the road and pick out another one."

In the distance, Sara heard the roar of the enormous tree as it fell, splitting the silence of the winter landscape. At first Sara had thought it was a result of yesterday's storm. This could happen, she knew. An old tree, laden with wet snow and weakened by strong winds, could just give way. But then she thought she heard voices. She strained to hear. Yes! Voices! People—people who would know where Pat Frewen's farm was, people who could help her find her way again! Tears raced down Sara's face as she started to run towards the source of the sound. Maybe she wouldn't die alone in the freezing snow, after all. Her heart lifted once more. This *was* turning out to be an adventure!

Archie Gillis patted the beautiful green spruce tenderly. "You're a real beauty," he murmured. "You'll bring a good price at the sawmill."

"I'd like to see *you* cut up at the sawmill, Archie Gillis! You and your stinking saws!"

Peg Bowen, known as the Witch of Avonlea, looked fiercer than usual as she strode out of her patchwork shack towards Archie Gillis and his beefy helpers. She puffed furiously on her pipe, and the men's boots she wore kicked up a drift of snow as she drilled along.

"Get off my land, you snake," hissed Peg, in Archie's face.

Archie stood his ground, although Peg Bowen, in full flight, was a formidable sight. She was wrapped in thick, dark, ragged shawls that whipped in the wind. A dirty red bandanna restrained her wiry gray hair and her black eyes blazed like coals. She shot a look at Jeb and Zeke. Instinctively, they stepped back. So did Rupert. Peg laughed defiantly, then turned her attention once again to Archie.

"Clear off my property," she ordered.

"*Your* property?" snarled Archie. "I got a licence to cut on this land. I should be orderin' you off!"

"Pa's right!" echoed Rupert, as bravely as he could.

Peg spoke quietly now, which was somehow even more frightening than when she shouted. She sounded reasonable, like a patient teacher, but her words were fueled by a furnace of anger.

"Let me give you a little history lesson. You haven't lived in Avonlea long enough to be ordering anyone around. When Mr. Van Der Veer owned the sawmill, he'd never have dreamed of taking trees this close to town, let alone the roof over my head. He had some common decency."

Archie wasn't going to be intimidated. "You can put your decency in your pipe and smoke it, you dragon. You're nothing but a squatter!"

Jeb and Zeke laughed nervously at Archie's audacity. Peg narrowed her eyes in hatred as she glared at the intruders, each in turn.

"May hyenas dance on your mothers' graves and may cherry stones jam your throats and choke you three shades of purple, you brutes! And you, Archie Gillis, may the motley, ragtag hockey team you coach lose every game you play this year! Now clear off, the lot of you!"

Jeb and Zeke turned, stumbling, and started to run. Rupert moved closer to his father.

"Jeb! Zeke!" shouted Archie. "Stand your ground!"

Peg roared with laughter as the large men scrambled up the hill, puffing and panting, their breath billowing out in frosty clouds.

Archie turned to Peg. "We'll be back, you witch. Make no mistake about that!"

"Another curse could be worse," whispered Peg, as she turned her back on Archie and Rupert and marched triumphantly back towards her cabin.

As Sara plowed through the last snowdrift, she caught just a flash of Archie and Rupert disappearing into the bush. In an instant, as Sara stood alone in the forest clearing, she realized where she was.

"Oh no," she groaned aloud. "I can't believe it." But there was no doubt about it. The rising smoke Sara had followed for the last half mile was drifting up from Peg Bowen's cabin!

Peg was about to enter the cabin when she sensed someone standing behind her. She spun around, thinking Archie and his crew might have returned. When she saw it was Sara, the dark look lifted from her face.

"Oh," she muttered, "it's only you."

Now that Sara had stopped moving, she realized how truly chilled she was.

"How's your cat?" inquired Peg. "Still licking at the butter dish at night?"

So that's why the butter always vanished at such a rate! But how did Peg know that? wondered Sara. Her teeth started to chatter.

"You look half-frozen, Sara Stanley. How long have you been lost?"

"I—I don't know. I'm trying to get to Pat Frewen's farm to get help to—"

"Save your breath," ordered Peg. "No point standing out here jawing. You'd better come in and get warmed up before you go anywhere else."

Sara hesitated. She knew she should speed along to Pat Frewen's, but she truly was chilled to the bone.

"I make a pretty good cup of tea, and you look like you could use it," announced Peg matter-of-factly. "I'm not going to eat you, you know," Peg assured her. "You look a bit thin, anyway." She laughed. "Just teasin' you, Sara."

Sara smiled weakly and followed Peg Bowen in the door.

Peg's cabin was surprisingly cozy and deliciously warm. A jolly pot-bellied stove glowed in the center of the single large room. Snug against one wall was a wooden table ringed by three mismatched chairs. The center of the table was graced by a vase of dried flowers, even prettier than the ones in the Rose Cottage parlor. Peg was very knowledgeable about preserving plants, and big bunches of dried herbs hung upside-down in one corner of the room.

Above a small bed was a long shelf, filled with books. For some reason, Sara had always thought Peg Bowen couldn't read. Now that she saw the well-worn volumes, she felt ashamed of that assumption. Three of Peg's cats were curled up on the small oval rug in front of the stove while two others were asleep on the bed. The sixth sat in front of Sara, regarding her suspiciously, his tail switching.

Peg filled a kettle with water she dipped up from a big wooden bucket by the door. "You hungry?" she asked, swinging the kettle onto the stove.

Sara realized she was famished, her breakfast bread-and-jam now just a distant memory.

"Well, yes, I guess I am," she admitted.

Peg reached into the cupboard. "Ever eaten bread baked in a tin?"

Just as Sara was about to answer, there was a rush of black wings and a loud screech. Sara screamed and ducked her head.

"Stop that, Merlin!" shouted Peg. "Darn crow, thinks every time I eat, he's goin' to eat. Get back on that perch this minute, Merlin, and I mean it. Away with you now."

With a flap and another scolding cry, Merlin flew to his high corner roost. No wonder Sara hadn't noticed him, way up there. He peered down at them with smoldering yellow eyes.

Sara had seen Merlin once before, when she'd come to ask Peg for special medicine for her friend Peter Craig. "I guess Merlin must like it here, he doesn't seem to fly away" said Sara.

"That's right, and you've seen Blackie, my three-legged dog? He's probably sleepin' under the bed." Sure enough, when Sara looked down she could just see the tip of Blackie's tail. As soon as he heard his name, his tail started to thump. Sara smiled.

Peg slapped the bottom of an old coffee tin smartly with her hand and a high, round loaf of bread popped out.

"I don't have an oven," explained Peg, "so I bake bread on top of the stove this way. Yup. I learned this little trick when I was up in the Yukon panning for gold."

"Holy smoke!" exclaimed Sara. "Did you really pan for gold?"

Peg picked up a large knife and started sawing at the bread. "Sure did. Found enough to stake me for two years, but then I went broke."

As Sara warmed up, she started feeling more at ease. "What did you do when you went broke?"

"I moved on."

"It's hard, isn't it," sighed Sara, "leaving your home and moving."

Peg poured strong, black tea into two thick, white mugs. "Nope. It doesn't matter where you live. As long as you're at home here—" she tapped her heart— "then you can live anywhere. In the summer I live by the sea, in the winter I live here. But I could be anywhere. It don't matter."

Peg placed the steaming mugs and a plate of buttered bread on the table. She sat down and sipped her tea enthusiastically, added two huge spoons of sugar and slurped again. Sara wrapped her hands around the mug, warming them. Then she, too, drank tea and munched on the "tin" bread, which was chewy but very tasty. The silence was broken only by the crackling of the stove.

Sitting this way with Peg Bowen, Sara suddenly realized that Peg wasn't nearly as old as she had thought. Sara had guessed Peg to be at least Aunt

Hetty's age, but up close, Sara could see she was considerably younger. And Peg had quite pretty eyes, very dark, but shot with amber. If she was thoroughly washed and "done up," she would be pretty, thought Sara. What a strange thought—Peg Bowen pretty.

Peg spoke, quietly. "You afraid of silence, Sara Stanley?"

Sara thought about it. "Sometimes."

Peg nodded her understanding. Three of the cats sprang up on the table and proceeded to greedily lick the butter off a piece of bread Peg offered them. Then Peg snapped her fingers and Merlin swooped down to join the picnic. Blackie limped over, followed by the other three cats, and the retinue was complete.

"I thought cats always killed birds," observed Sara.

"Not if they're brought up together," countered Peg. A fierce look clouded her face. "Men can be brutes," she hissed. "That tree out there? Archie Gillis thinks it's just a piece of wood, but it was a home for birds, and insects, and squirrels, and now that home has been cut away from 'em. Brutes!"

Sara considered this. "I thought you said it doesn't matter where you live."

"That's true," confirmed Peg. "But the choice has gotta be yours, not someone else's."

Sara nodded and watched Merlin tear at the bread with his skillful beak. My goodness, she

thought, Aunt Hetty would have a fit if she saw this!
Speaking of Aunt Hetty...!

"Miss Bowen, I really must be going," announced
Sara. "My aunts are counting on me and Hetty's
sick and I must fetch Pat Frewen so that he can fix
our chimney."

Peg rose from the table and moved towards the
corner. "You're a lot closer to Jasper Dale's than Pat
Frewen's. Jasper can fix your chimney. I'll walk you
there." Peg reached up and pulled down a stalk of
dried herbs. "By the way, does your Aunt Hetty
have the flu?"

Sara's eyes widened. "H-have the flu? Yes, I think
so. I mean, she's sneezing something terrific and she
looks feverish."

"Camomile tea is good for fever, and pine nuts
will ease a cough. A little warm almond oil rubbed
on her chest should help, too." Peg gathered the
medicines up and tied them securely in a clean rag.
She stuffed the bundle into her pocket. Then she
picked up her pipe and turned to Sara.

"Ready?"

Sara nodded, and they moved towards the door.
Peg paused.

"And by the way, it's about time you called me
Peg. I'm not Miss Bowen."

Sara was startled. "You're married?"

"That's not what I said," declared Peg. "I just don't believe in all this Miss and Mrs. business. A person's a person and that's the end of it."

With that observation, Peg Bowen sailed out the door, her pipe clenched between her teeth.

Chapter Three

Sara and Peg clomped along in companionable silence through the deep, soft snow. Sara realized that she had managed to get completely turned in the wrong direction on her earlier trek, and she was grateful for Miss Bowen's—Peg's—guidance now. It was a crisp, clean winter day, dazzling, with no wind. From time to time Sara spotted animal tracks cut in the whiteness. Peg would gesture and say, "Rabbits," or "Foxes." Once, to Sara's delight, she whispered, "Deer."

Sara loved the woods, but she didn't have Peg's deep understanding of its animals and plants, and the turn of the seasons and what that meant. Until today, Sara had thought that Peg Bowen had nothing to offer but a rather odd view of the world and some intriguing magical talents. Now she was beginning to think that Peg had wisdom and insight, too.

Peg stopped abruptly and started kicking snow aside to clear a small area. "Rest," she ordered.

"But there's nothing to sit on!" protested Sara. Peg laughed and squatted down on her haunches.

"Sit on your shins," directed Peg, "Indian style."

Somewhat reluctantly, Sara followed Peg's example, clearing an area and squatting. It was quite comfortable, after all.

Peg closed her eyes. After a moment, she spoke. "Hetty's worked herself into a state about Muriel Stacey's visit," she observed, as though speaking to herself.

"I know," replied Sara. "I wish I understood why."

Peg shifted slightly. "Hetty and Muriel became best friends at teacher's college in Charlottetown, and your Aunt Hetty's not one to make friends easily."

Sara nodded but said nothing, hoping her silence would prompt Peg to go on.

"Your grandparents were still alive then, and the King farm was a busy, bubbling place. There were box socials and the sewing circle and the Literary Society used to meet there. All the young folk would gather at the King place, and—"

"Then you must have known my mother, Ruth King!" cried Sara.

"No."

"But you must have *seen* her," insisted Sara. "What was she like?"

Peg spoke softly. "I really didn't know her, Sara. But what I saw of her makes me think she was a dreamy one. Off in a world of her own half the time. I can only go by what I saw, though. I was never invited to join in."

Sara looked down. "I'm sorry."

"Don't be! I wanted to be on my own. People used to call me 'Strange Little Peg,' even then. I didn't care a fig."

Sara felt a pang. Of course Peg must have cared. But it was confusing—wanting to be part of a group, yet wanting to be your very own person.

"Anyway," continued Peg, "Hetty used to bring Muriel home with her for summer holidays. I'd see 'em at the beach, laughin' and walkin' along the shore. They graduated and then..." Peg paused and reached in her pocket for her pipe.

"And then what?" pressed Sara.

Peg lit her pipe and puffed vigorously. "Then only Hetty and Muriel really know what happened. One of them will have to tell you."

"But Aunt Hetty won't talk about it!" wailed Sara. "Please, please, tell me what happened. Please!" Sara's hunch, that Hetty's grudge against Muriel went back a long, long way, was growing by the minute.

Peg stood up and, once again, started tramping through the snow towards Jasper Dale's place, Golden Milestone. Sara scrambled to keep up.

"Please tell me, Peg! If you don't, I'll—I'll—"

"You'll what?" challenged Peg.

Sara grabbed the first thought within reach. "I'll tell everyone that you're not a witch. I'll tell everyone that you're just a normal person! That we had tea together and everything."

Peg started to laugh, a great, rolling laugh. Then she stopped and shook her head.

"You are a very brave girl, Sara Stanley, to threaten someone with my powers. But I'll tell you one more thing. Hetty and Muriel's break had to do with jealousy over a boyfriend."

"Oh," exclaimed Sara, "an affair of the heart! I should have known. Of course, Hetty would be upset if Muriel's beau intruded on their friendship."

Peg smiled slightly. "Oh no, Sara. It weren't Muriel's boyfriend, it were Hetty's. And it weren't Romney Penhallow."

Sara stopped dead in her tracks. Hetty once had a boyfriend, other than Romney Penhallow?! Two boyfriends!! She couldn't believe her ears. Hetty? Prim, plain, prickly-as-a-pincushion Hetty?!

"Sara, you look like a stunned toad," laughed Peg. "And, being a witch, I know a thing or two about toads!"

Sara tried to gather her thoughts. "Hetty's other boyfriend? What was his name? What happened?" she called after Peg. But Peg had moved away, and Sara's questions were left floating in the nippy air.

Jasper Dale's house was a fantasy of ice and snow. Golden Milestone was one of those Avonlea houses decorated with an elaborate gingerbread trim gracing its eaves and windows. Long, gleaming icicles stretched from the corners of the roof towards the ground. Just as Sara opened the snow-topped gate, she spotted Jasper at the back of the house, loping towards the barn.

"Mr. Dale!" she called, but he didn't hear her.

"Well, at least we know he's here," confirmed Peg, "so I'll leave you now. I want to get home, in case Archie Gillis comes back."

Sara nodded. "Miss Bow—" Peg raised a warning eyebrow. "Peg, thank you for rescuing me."

"You're welcome," muttered Peg, reaching into her pocket. She pulled out the bundle of medicines and handed it to Sara. "Hetty won't want to take these, but you'll find a way to persuade her."

"I will?"

Peg offered nothing more as she turned and tramped off, her pipe smoke curling up into the winter afternoon.

Sara plowed her way, through deep snow, up the path leading to the barn.

"Mr. Dale?" she called.

As she approached the barn, she could hear squawking sounds—very loud squawking sounds. Sara leaned against the large barn door and pushed her way into the darkness. The familiar scent of hay and the sweet, warm breath of cows in their stalls reassured Sara as she walked towards the source of the uproar.

A kerosene lamp looped over a nail on a beam illuminated a chaotic scene at the back of the barn. Jasper Dale, looking even more disheveled than usual, was struggling with a white goose who was screeching resentfully. Every time Jasper tried to catch the huge bird, it squirted out of his arms, flapping and screaming. Sara's eyes widened.

"Mr. Dale! What's going on?"

Clearly, this was not a time for lengthy explanations. "Get in here, Sara!" Jasper commanded. "Give me a hand!"

Sara paused. For one thing, she was quite startled to hear Jasper speaking in such a rough un-Jasper-like fashion. For another, Sara was frightened of geese. Once, when she was a little girl visiting a farm, a large goose had chased her, its big yellow bill clacking and snapping as it flapped its great wings and honked its disapproval of her trespassing. Sara had been terrified and had run screaming to her mother. The goose chased her right to the door, its button-black eyes shining. Ever since then, she had stayed as far away from geese as she could, and now, now she was being told that she had to help catch one!

"Sara!" hollered Jasper, through the clamor, "Help me, for heaven's sake!"

Reluctantly, Sara joined Jasper. "What am I supposed to do?" she shouted. "I don't know what to do!"

"Just block him from that side of the pen!" yelled Jasper. "He's got a broken wing, I think. I just want to get a good look at him. Whoa! Whoa!"

The terrified goose, honking in panic, turned and started to run straight towards Sara. He looked bigger than Sara had thought, as he scrabbled and flapped along the frozen earth.

"Stop him, Sara!" called Jasper. "Grab him!"

"I can't!" howled Sara. Then she spun round and ran, her heart pounding, past the startled cows and out the barn door. She didn't stop until she reached the back door of Jasper Dale's house.

Couldn't she do anything right? Sara thought, as she stood gasping, the cold air stabbing her throat. First she had got stupidly lost, now she'd shown herself to be a coward, and she still hadn't accomplished what she had promised her aunts she would—to get someone to fix the chimney of Rose Cottage! Sara moaned out loud. What was wrong with her?

"There, that should do just f-f-fine," declared Jasper, as he set a splint on the goose's broken wing. Sara nodded, too humiliated to say anything. Jasper had managed to catch the bird, calm him and bring him into the warmth of Golden Milestone's big, old kitchen. So far, Jasper hadn't commented on Sara's panicky exit from the barn.

"P-pass me that cheese, will you, S-S-Sara?" asked Jasper, as he pushed his spectacles back up his long nose.

Sara handed Jasper a fine bit of cheddar from the side cupboard. Jasper offered it to the goose, and the injured bird snapped it up and greedily gulped it down.

"What happened to him?" asked Sara, trying to recover her confidence.

"I d-d-don't really know. There was some k-k-kind of uproar in the barn. P-p-poor fellow broke his wing."

"He likes the cheese," noted Sara.

"My m-mother used to say cheese is like candy," stammered Jasper, "t-t-to a goose, that is. But t-tell me, Sara Stanley, what brings you out on such a cold d-d-day?"

So Sara told him about the blocked chimney, and the desperate situation at Rose Cottage, and although

Jasper asserted that he was no expert on chimneys, he promised he would do what he could.

As Jasper gave his earnest offer of help, Sara felt a wave of shame. She had failed to help Jasper when he had needed it most. This was not a good start to the new year.

Chapter Four

"Hetty!" Olivia called. "Sara's back!" Olivia hugged Sara close. "We were getting so worried, but you're home now, thank goodness!"

"Sara," croaked Hetty, coming down the hall, "where on earth have you been?!"

"Well," sighed Sara, "it's a long story."

Hetty exploded into a coughing fit and waved her hand feebly, indicating that Sara's tale would have to wait. Sara was just as glad.

"Hello, O-Olivia," offered Jasper, as he stamped the snow off his boots just outside the door. "Hetty, you look—o-off-color, I must say."

Hetty, her face buried in a handkerchief, shook her head in muffled acknowledgment. Olivia reached up and started to tuck away bits of stray hair that had escaped from her bun.

"Oh, dear, Jasper, my goodness, we told Sara to fetch Pat Frewen to fix the pig, I mean to fix the chimney!" Olivia laughed merrily. She always glowed when Jasper Dale was around, no matter what the circumstance. And he always glowed back.

"W-well, Sara got turned around and ended up at m-m-my place," explained Jasper. "I hope I can h-h-help."

"Oh, I'm sure you can, Jasper," confirmed Olivia, warmly.

Sara was relieved that Olivia's focus was on Jasper, and not her. The thought of relating her mounting list of failures and fears to her aunts was not appealing.

Hetty, her coughing subsided, seized control of the situation.

"You'd better come along, Jasper," she directed, hoarsely "As you can see, we're almost frozen in here. Sara, you look pale. While Jasper investigates the chimney, you'd best get something to eat, my girl. Olivia, fetch the long broom from the pantry for Jasper. Olivia, are you listening to me?"

Olivia grinned at Sara, a little wickedly. "Of course, Hetty. I always listen to you, don't I?"

Having finished relating to Olivia and Hetty the story of how she got lost, and found, by Peg Bowen, Sara stuffed the last of the gingerbread cake into her mouth. She washed it down with a big drink of icy milk and then burped, rather loudly. Aunt Hetty did not look amused.

"Excuse yourself, Sara," she prompted.

"Excuse me," Sara said, as Hetty removed Sara's plate from the table.

Overhead, Jasper Dale's footsteps thudded on the roof as he positioned himself to clear the chimney that ran up from the kitchen stove.

"That's good," shouted Olivia, craning her neck up the chimney, trying to see Jasper. "Just start in, Jasper! Just start poking that broom down! Let's see what happens!" She sounded quite gay about the whole thing.

"S-stand by below!" hollered Jasper.

"Really, Olivia," chided Hetty, "this isn't a—a magic lantern show or some such entertainment. We have a serious situation on our hands."

Sara smiled. It was good to be home.

"Aunt Hetty, may I have another piece of ginger-bread cake?" she asked.

"That was the last of it, Sara. I can't do any more baking until the stove is working again, and then, as you know, baking for Muriel's visit is my priority. Oh dear," lamented Hetty, "this time tomorrow she'll be here! And there's so much to do..."

Hetty plunked down beside Sara at the kitchen table. She took out a handkerchief and blew her nose, forcefully. Suddenly, Sara remembered! She reached into her pocket and produced the bundle Peg Bowen had prepared. She placed it in front of Hetty.

"There," announced Sara.

Hetty looked wary. "There what?"

"There is the cure for your cold, Aunt Hetty. Open it."

Suspicious, Hetty prodded the bundle apart. "This is just a pile of dried weeds or somesuch. Where did you get this?"

"From Peg Bowen," replied Sara.

"*Miss* Bowen," corrected Hetty. "She may be extremely odd, but she must be spoken of with proper respect."

"But she told me to call her Peg, Aunt Hetty— honestly!"

Just as Hetty was about to respond, a great cloud of soot billowed out from the stove into the kitchen.

"Oh dear, Jasper!" exclaimed Olivia, coughing and sputtering as she tried to block the rolling filth with a large old blanket she was holding. Hetty and Sara ran to help her, and they managed to contain the damage somewhat.

"I think that's g-g-got it!" shouted Jasper, down the chimney. "There was a build-up of s-soot about halfway down and—" His explanation trailed off into a cough, as some of the soot drifted back up.

"Work your way along the roof to the chimney over the fireplace in the parlor, Jasper!" called Olivia, as the soot settled. "I'll meet you there!" She turned to Hetty and Sara, her face and arms now streaked with black.

"Olivia, you look a sight!" exclaimed Hetty.

Olivia smiled. "I'm not the only one," she observed, sweetly, as she flounced from the kitchen and headed for the parlor.

Hetty and Sara peered into the small kitchen mirror. Olivia was right. They, too, were streaked with soot.

"I look like the Little Chimney Sweep!" declared Sara, pleased. She liked the thought of looking like a character in one of her favorite stories.

Hetty shook her head, dipped a cloth in water and attempted to wipe the oily dirt from her face and arms. She passed the cloth to Sara, and then she started to cough once again. Sara picked up the little bottle of almond oil from the medicine bundle.

"Aunt Hetty, if you warm this and rub it on your chest, it will help your cold. Peg Bowen really does know a lot of things. Truly."

"Such as?" she asked, haughtily.

"Such as that you and Muriel Stacey used to be best friends!" Sara blurted out.

Hetty looked startled at this outburst. "I beg your pardon?"

"Yes," continued Sara, boldly. "And that Muriel used to come to Avonlea for holidays, and that you used to walk together on the beach, and—"

Hetty held up a warning hand. "Listen to me, Sara. I know you're a very curious child, and that's a quality to be admired—in a student. But these are personal matters, and adult personal matters, at that."

"But Aunt Hetty, you're the one who's always telling me I'm growing up too fast," protested Sara. "I *am* growing up, you know!"

"Miss Peg Bowen does not know what happened between Muriel Stacey and me, and I strongly suggest that you not pursue the matter."

"So something *did* happen!" declared Sara, triumphantly.

"Sara, I will not have this, do you understand? *Do you understand?*"

Hetty collapsed into a desperate coughing fit, and all her fierceness seemed to drain away. Sara took Hetty's dry, hot hand.

"Please, Aunt Hetty, let me make you a cup of camomile tea. I can heat a little bit of water over a candle and I'm sure it will help you. Please? At least try it. I know it's something new, but after all, you're the one who always says 'A teaspoon of courage sweetens the cup of life.'"

Hetty, miserable, could only nod her agreement. "You are persistent," she rasped.

"Just like you, Aunt Hetty."

While Hetty sipped her camomile tea, Sara joined Olivia in the parlor to offer what help she could. Jasper was tromping and pounding on the roof, and there seemed to be more sound than progress on the chimney-clearing front.

"It sounds like all Santa's reindeer are clog-dancing, doesn't it, Aunt Olivia?" asked Sara, as she helped Olivia hold up the blanket across the fireplace opening.

Olivia laughed. "I don't know, Sara. I've never heard a reindeer clog-dance."

Jasper's voice drifted down. "There's something b-b-big up here!"

Olivia and Sara exchanged a puzzled look. Olivia strained to see up the chimney. "What is it, Jasper?"

"I don't k-know. Just—"

"We're ready for anything!" Sara called up.

Hetty bustled in, looking somewhat recovered. "I've managed to get the fire going in the kitchen, now what's all the racket about?" she demanded.

"Reindeer clog-dancing," teased Sara.

"Something big," offered Olivia.

"Whoa!" hollered Jasper, down the chimney. "Stand clear!! There's a b-b-big nest, or—whoa!!"

With that, a rolling, spinning blur of twigs and sticks and bits of branch, clouded in soot, came hurtling down the chimney! Olivia and Sara screamed and instinctively leapt back as the spiky mass landed at their feet, on the parlor floor.

"Good Lord!" squealed Hetty. "What have we here?"

What they had was obviously a big nest, still largely intact. Warily, they approached it.

"Are you al-all right down there?" called Jasper.

"Come back down, Jasper," instructed Olivia. "This is extremely interesting."

Sara's eyes widened. "What is it?"

"It's a squirrel's nest," came the confident answer, from the direction of the door.

Everyone wheeled around. There stood a handsome woman with a rather large nose and penetrating brown eyes, dressed in a sturdy, dark-green coat trimmed in gray fur.

"Muriel!" cried Hetty, clutching her throat in dismay. Sara gasped.

"Muriel?" echoed Olivia, feebly.

"Well, of course it's me. Hetty, my train arrived an hour ago. I waited for you at the station, but..."

Hetty looked stricken. "Oh, dear, Muriel, you're not supposed to arrive until tomorrow!"

"No, no," countered Muriel. "I said I would arrive on January the second and commence the school inspection on the third. Today *is* the second, Hetty."

Hetty, streaked with soot and her nose dripping, looked quite undone.

Sara was struck once more by Muriel Stacey's single overriding feature—her extraordinary voice. It was deeply and exquisitely pitched, creamy and smooth, like chocolate sauce. It gave her whole presence a kind of warmth and, yes, even nobility. Hetty's voice, especially today, was like a cracked teacup.

Olivia glided forward, extending a grimy hand. "How do you do, Miss Stacey."

Muriel waved vaguely at Olivia, deftly declining the grubby handshake. Hetty spoke again, trying to establish her authority in this awkward situation.

"And of course you know Sara—Sara—" Unfortunately for Hetty and everyone concerned, a violent, resonating sneeze overtook her, shaking her slender body with hurricane-like force.

Sara stepped forward and addressed Muriel. "How are you, Miss Stacey?"

"I'm rather weary, if truth be told," said Muriel.

As Jasper came stamping into the parlor, Muriel drew back. Jasper grinned, and his teeth gleamed brightly against the backdrop of his soot-streaked face.

"I-I-I did it! Those squirrels thought they'd found the p-p-perfect place to hibernate for the winter, but they were wr-wr-wrong."

"Muriel," croaked Hetty, "this is Jasper Dale. Jasper, this is Miss Muriel Stacey, the school superintendent."

"Pl-pl-pleased..." Jasper, flushed with his chimney-clearing success, had failed to notice Muriel when he entered the room. Now, as was always the case in the presence of strangers, his stammer struck him down.

"I didn't think Avonlea was of a size to have a resident chimney sweep," observed Muriel.

"Oh, Jasper isn't a chimney sweep," volunteered Sara, brightly. "He's really a very talented photographer and inventor."

Muriel sniffed. Jasper looked miserable.

"Well," rasped Hetty, "we'd better get you up to your room, Muriel. Sara, perhaps you would help Miss Stacey with her luggage. Jasper, if you would be so kind as to remove the—the nest, and Olivia, perhaps you could put on the kettle for tea?"

Poor Aunt Hetty, thought Sara, as she dragged Muriel's suitcase up the stairs. She'd never seen her looking so bedraggled, and so off-balance. And whatever the reasons were, Sara, too, was having second thoughts about Muriel Stacey. She seemed to be snobby and rather ungracious. Sara pushed open the door to the guest bedroom at the top of the stairs.

"This is your room, Miss Stacey," she announced, rather formally.

Muriel nodded. "Well, it's better than a hotel, I suppose."

Sara bit her tongue, but offered no comment. Hetty had often reminded her not to be rude to her elders.

Muriel removed her large hat and set it on the bed. She turned to Sara.

"I'm sorry, Sara. That was an untoward remark. It's just that it's been a long day."

"Yes, it has been a long day, Miss Stacey" replied Sara, haughtily, as she closed the door and walked downstairs into the sooty chaos of the living room.

Chapter Five

Felix King's plump face was pink with excitement. "Jumping Jehoshaphat! A squirrel's nest right in the parlor! Did the squirrels run off?"

"No," replied Sara, "they were asleep, curled up into furry little balls, and they just stayed that way. At least that's what they were doing when Jasper took the nest away."

Cecily looked up from the baby bootie she was laboriously knitting. "Aunt Hetty must have had three fits," she observed, with a little smile.

"Now, I don't think that's a very kind thing to say about your Aunt Hetty," scolded Aunt Janet, fanning herself with the Christmas edition of the Avonlea *Chronicle* as she sat in her favorite big chair in the corner of the homey kitchen.

Poor Aunt Janet, thought Sara. She looks even more pregnant than she did when I saw her Christmas Day, and that was just a week ago. The baby looks like it's sitting on her lap!

"Well," mused Felix, "them squirrels must have been hibernating, that's what they must have been doing."

"*Those* squirrels," corrected Felicity, as she wrapped a large date loaf in a fresh tea towel. "Really, Felix, I think you speak that way just to provoke me!"

"Maybe I does, and maybe I doesn't," answered Felix, with a wicked gleam in his eye.

Sara laughed. Felix could be the very devil.

"Oh, please children," begged Janet, "I can't bear any squabbling today."

"You all heard Mother," reinforced Felicity, primly. "Now, Sara, what else can we send off with you for the 'Muriel Stacey Rescue Effort'?"

"Whatever you can spare—baking, cold meat, anything," replied Sara. "Aunt Olivia told me to get whatever I could beg, borrow or steal for dinner tonight, and for breakfast tomorrow."

Janet smiled. "Well, dear, we're family, so it's a matter of borrowing, not begging or steal—" Suddenly, Janet's face twisted with pain.

"Mother!" cried Felicity, springing to her side. "Is it time?"

Felix, Cecily and Sara stared, wide-eyed.

Janet shifted in the chair, trying to find a more comfortable position. "No, no," she assured them all, "it's just Baby King's way of making his presence felt. As if I didn't know he, or she, was there already!" She sat back as the twinge subsided. Sara breathed a sigh of relief.

To be honest, she wanted to be as far away as possible when Aunt Janet gave birth. The whole process, or what she knew of it, frightened Sara. She'd never seen a woman in labor, but once she had witnessed the birth of a calf, and had found it a terrifying experience—the bellowing cow wild-eyed with pain, the blood, the strange convulsive movements. As a matter of fact, it had so alarmed Sara that she had fled from the barn, and hadn't gone back until word came that the calf was alive and well and on its feet. She could only imagine how stupendously awful a human birth must be!

From time to time, as the life of Avonlea unfolded, she heard whispers about the matter. "Poor Tillie Crawford had a ghastly labor," Sara had once overheard Hetty whisper to Olivia. "Well, let's pray she doesn't die from childbed fever," answered Olivia, gravely. Tillie Crawford had survived, but there were others who hadn't. Two years ago Harriet Wilson had died in childbirth, and she was only twenty-one! Such losses brought sadness to the whole community, as young men were left alone to care for an infant, and often other children, as well. Sara loved babies, but she didn't like to think about how they arrived.

Felicity, on the other hand, took all this child-birth business in stride. Now, as she brought her mother a cup of tea, she looked terribly efficient and grown-up.

"*After* the little one's born," Sara volunteered, "I'll sing to it and cuddle it. I'll tell it wonderful stories."

"There's a lot more to babies than just singing and cuddling, Sara," cautioned Felicity. "But of course, how could you possibly know? You're an only child. I'm an expert on babies. I helped to raise both Cecily and Felix."

"Felicity," Sara reminded her, "as I remember, we both took care of Abigail and Malcolm's baby when we found him last year."

Blithely ignoring this fact, Felicity turned to her mother. "When it's time for the baby to be born, I'll be indispensable to you, Mother," she announced, in ringing tones.

Janet smiled wanly. "Well, I hope so, dear. I'll need all the help I can get. After all, it's been ten years since I gave birth!"

"We'll help the baby be born, too!" chorused Felix and Cecily. Sara said nothing and hoped no one noticed.

Felicity returned to the pantry and discovered half a cold roast of beef, which she expertly wrapped and placed in a basket along with the date loaf, slices of cold turkey and a large bowl of jellied salad. She tied the large hamper with strong cord and handed it to Sara. "This should keep the wolf from the door," she proclaimed.

"I'll take some of that!" declared Alec, as he wiped his snowy boots on the rug and entered the cheery warmth of the kitchen.

"Daddy, you're back! You're back!" cried the children.

"With a full load of wood, as promised," said Alec, giving Janet a concerned look. He spoke gently as he leaned down and kissed her on the forehead. "And how's my girl? Still holding on?"

"Nothing else I can do."

He patted her shoulder, tenderly.

"Hello, Uncle Alec," chirped Sara.

"Sara, what brings you out on such a cold day? Are my sisters getting even more impossible to live with?" He laughed, enjoying his own joke.

"Alec, really," scolded Janet, "Hetty and Olivia aren't ogres, you know."

"Ain't they though!" exclaimed Felix, in such a startling way that everyone had to laugh.

"Now before you take off your coat, Alec dear," instructed Janet, "I want you to drive Sara back to Rose Cottage. She's had a very tiring day, poor child. But I'm sure she'll tell you all about it, won't you, Sara?"

Sara was beginning to wonder if this day would ever end, between the day itself and all the telling.

"Well, Sara's quite the little storyteller," smiled Alec, "so I look forward to that."

So Sara once again bundled up, thanked Aunt Janet and Felicity for the hamper and hopped up beside Uncle Alec on the sleigh. As the horses stamped and snorted in the frigid air, setting the sleighbells tinkling merrily, Alec carefully wrapped a heavy blanket around Sara's legs. Then he snapped the reins smartly and they trotted briskly off in the direction of the wintry lemon sun, which was sinking low in the western sky.

As Alec and Sara neared the lane to Rose Cottage, a large sledge approached them, fishtailing along the snowy road, obviously trying to make speed. The crack of the driver's whip as he urged the four horses on across the icy fields.

"There's a man in a hurry," declared Alec.

Sara recognized the driver instantly. "That's Archie Gillis! The horrible man I told you about, the fiend who was cutting trees near Peg Bowen's."

Alec chuckled. "Now, Sara, he's not my favorite addition to Avonlea, but he's not a fiend, either. Anyway, friend or fiend, Archie Gillis looks like he's got trouble."

"Good!" pronounced Sara.

"Whoa, whoa there," called Alec, and the horses stamped to a standstill. Archie, with Rupert sitting beside him, approached and reined in his team.

"Anything wrong, Gillis?" inquired Alec.

"Had a bit of an accident down the road. My men were hauling a log and the cursed sledge overturned." He gestured to the back of the sledge, where Zeke Sloan and Jeb Ryan were lying, moaning. "We're taking them to Doc Blair's. I think we're looking at a broken arm and maybe a broken ankle."

"Aha!" trumpeted Sara. "You should have listened to Peg Bowen. You should never have cut down her tree!"

Archie Gillis's eyes narrowed. "I know you, you little troublemaker. You're in league with that old witch. You were part of the curse, you little scoundrel!"

"She's not old!" argued Sara. "And I'm not a scoundrel!"

"You are so!" bellowed Rupert.

Alec held up a warning hand. "Wait, wait a minute, all of you. The most important thing right now is to get Zeke and Jeb to the doctor's. Can you manage, Gillis, or can we help?"

Archie Gillis's face darkened. "We can manage without your help, Alec King, thank you very much. You just mind your business and I'll mind mine." With that, he cracked the whip and the sledge sliced past them, cutting sharply through the snow.

"Well," announced Alec, "there goes Archie Gillis's hockey team! With Zeke and Jeb out of commission, the Avonlea Avengers have lost their two best players. As the new coach, Gillis certainly has his work cut out."

Now, if there was one thing Sara was spectacularly uninterested in, it was ice hockey. She thought it was a boring game, with people whizzing up and down the ice, chasing a wooden puck, crashing into each other for no apparent purpose. Perhaps part of Sara's distaste for the sport was the fact that she didn't skate. To be completely accurate, Sara *couldn't* skate. When she was a little girl, her family had moved frequently, and often spent winters in sunny places. So, between one thing and another,

Sara was that distinct oddity—a Canadian child who couldn't skate!

Alec turned to Sara. "Now what's all this about a curse, Sara?"

Sara shrugged her shoulders. She didn't want to get into a discussion about Peg Bowen's magic powers with Uncle Alec, who was, as Sara put it, "as practical as a pudding." A good tactic was to switch the subject.

"Uncle Alec," Sara inquired, "did Aunt Hetty ever have a boyfriend other than Romney Penhallow? I mean earlier, when she was at teachers' college?"

He paused for a moment. "Oh, I don't think so, Sara. She never was—well, Hetty's always been pretty independent."

"You're sure?"

Alec tapped his forehead, searching for an answer. "You know, I think once she did bring a young man home from Charlottetown, but I was just a boy and I didn't notice such things. But I think his name was—John."

Sara gripped Alec's arm in excitement. "John! What a splendid name! What was he like? Was he handsome, clever, funny? Could he dance? Did he like to read? Was he truly, truly in love with Aunt Hetty? And was she truly, truly in love with him? Oh, Uncle Alec, tell me everything, please!"

Alec couldn't help but laugh at Sara's impassioned questions. "Sara, I know you're going to be disappointed to hear this, but I really don't remember anything. It was a long time ago. It's all pretty fuzzy."

"Grown-ups never remember anything important," moaned Sara. "Don't you even know what happened to him? Did he leave Hetty, or did she leave him, or what, Uncle Alec?"

But there was no more information to be cajoled from Uncle Alec, and Sara was left with many more questions than answers. But at least she now knew that John, if that was his name, had actually been in Avonlea, and that Hetty had cared enough for him to bring him home to meet her stern parents. Sara sighed. As the poet said, the course of true love never did run smooth.

Chapter Six

Sara awoke early with the knowledge that holidays were over and today was a school day, and no mistake about it. Then she remembered—today was Inspection Day! Hetty's teaching career was in Muriel Stacey's hands! Or, rather, it was going to be in Muriel Stacey's report. Rose Cottage was quiet as Sara flung off her covers, dressed quickly and slipped down the stairs to the kitchen.

The last time Muriel had visited Avonlea, Olivia had written up her visit for the *Chronicle*, and everyone in town had read it. Olivia's article had compared Muriel and Hetty, and though Olivia had meant to point out her sister's good sense and practical nature, Hetty did emerge as rather—well, severe. Muriel Stacey, on the other hand, was clearly worldly and sophisticated. For example, when quizzed about their "beauty routines," Hetty had stated that plain soap and water were just fine, thank you very much. However, Muriel preferred English powder and French night cream. French night cream! How much more elegant could you get! Another difference was breakfast. Hetty favored unsalted oatmeal porridge, while Muriel liked to dine on warm, buttered muffins, gently spread with apple butter. And, in fact, muffins were the reason that Sara had arisen early. She was going to help Hetty out by making a fresh batch for Muriel Stacey's breakfast.

After shooing Topsy away from the butter dish and piling fresh coals on top of the glowing embers, Sara sat down at the kitchen table to read the recipe. Sara was well aware that her culinary abilities were, as Felicity was fond of pointing out, "lacking." Basically, Sara told herself, it was because baking and cooking just didn't interest her. That was true, as far as it went, but the heart of the matter, Sara felt, was that she just didn't have the knack. She refused to call it a talent, because talent was something reserved for great *artistes*. But whatever you called it, Sara wasn't very adept at matters of the kitchen. And even though Rachel Lynde had taught her a thing or two when they were quarantined together at Alexander Abraham's farm, a thing or two wasn't enough. But surely this morning, she thought, with concentration and effort, she could produce a batch of fresh, sweet muffins.

"Two cups of sifted flour," Sara chanted aloud, as though casting a magic spell. Just as she was about to measure them out, Hetty came sweeping into the kitchen. She was completely washed, fully dressed and wound as tight as a new top at a birthday party.

"Sara, what are you doing there, child? You're getting flour all over the kitchen!" As Hetty fussed about the kitchen getting water to prepare tea, measuring out oatmeal and setting out milk and sugar, she continued her monologue.

"Now what I want you to do is set the dining-room table with the best china and don't argue with me. I know it's only breakfast but I want things done properly. We'll wake Muriel in half an hour and that should give us time to get everything ready. Don't just stand there, child, with your mouth agape, do as I say!"

"But Aunt Hetty," wailed Sara, trying to concentrate as she measured out the sugar, "I'm making muffins for Miss Stacey's breakfast. You must remember how much she likes them."

Hetty swiped at her nose with a lace-trimmed handkerchief and kept moving. Clearly, her cold had improved, and Sara was convinced that Peg Bowen's camomile tea had done the trick.

"I'm glad to see your cold's better, Aunt Hetty," offered Sara.

"I don't have time to be ill, Sara, and you don't have time to be trying to make muffins. And no, I haven't the faintest idea whether or not Muriel likes them."

Olivia entered the kitchen, looking exceptionally pretty in a yellow-flowered day dress. "Oh, surely you remember the article I wrote, Hetty. You said you liked oatmeal and Muriel said she adored muffins."

"Adored muffins?" repeated Hetty, stiffly.

"You were quite upset about the article, Hetty," said Olivia, gently. "And so was I."

Hetty shook her head, as though ridding herself of a meddlesome mosquito. "Oh, I suppose I remember something or other, but what's that got to do with the price of cotton in Cornwall? Sara, I asked you to set the dining-room table!"

"I'll set it," volunteered Olivia, "Sara's almost finished mixing her muffins. Hetty, dear, do try and relax. Everything will be fine."

"I am relaxed!" squawked Hetty. "I am relaxed! Anyone can see that!"

"Good morning, everyone. My, what a hive of activity." Muriel Stacey's smooth tones wafted across the turmoil in the kitchen. "Are those muffins I see, Sara?"

"Yes, Miss Stacey," replied Sara, as she popped the muffins in the oven.

"What a thoughtful gesture," offered Muriel, warmly. Sara could see that a good night's sleep had done Muriel a world of good. She seemed much friendlier than she had yesterday.

"Good morning, Hetty, how's that dreadful cold of yours?" inquired Muriel.

"Improved. Thank you. How did you sleep?"

"Terribly well, I'm happy to relate. It must be the country air. Charlottetown just doesn't have this air. You always said, Hetty, that there was no air like Avonlea air."

"I did?"

"Yes, of course you did, Hetty. I always thought that was part of why you came back here after you finished teachers' college, instead of accepting that appointment in Halifax."

Halifax? Sara was surprised to hear this. It had never entered her head that Hetty had considered teaching anywhere other than Avonlea. Avonlea was her home, so of course she would return after her training. Wouldn't she?

"Halifax?" echoed Sara. "You almost went to Halifax!"

"No, I didn't almost go to Halifax," retorted Hetty, dismissively. "I hope you're watching the time on those muffins, Sara. Fifteen minutes and they're done."

"Hetty had a very special friend who lived in Halifax at the time," disclosed Muriel, somewhat slyly.

Hetty glared at her. "How dare you, Muriel Stacey! You, of all people!"

Suddenly, Sara knew. As clear as a June day, Sara knew!

"Was his name John, Aunt Hetty?"

Hetty shot Sara an arrow of a look. "That," she declared with quiet dignity, "is none of your concern."

So it *was* John! thought Sara. It must have been a truly passionate affair of the heart for Hetty to react so angrily, even all these years later.

"Hetty," said Muriel, "it was a long time ago. Couldn't we—"

Hetty cut her off sharply. "Breakfast will be served in the dining room. Please seat yourselves."

As the three ladies settled at the table, Sara slid the tray of muffins out of the oven. They looked splendid—golden and tempting. Success! She nested them in a basket lined with a cheerful red-checkered napkin and brought them to the table.

"Well, Sara," declared Hetty, "those look very nice, I must say."

"Hmmm," purred Muriel, as she buttered one of the steaming muffins.

Sara waited, anxiously, as Muriel bit into it. A most peculiar look crossed Muriel's face as she carefully chewed the first bite.

"Very—interesting," observed Muriel, as she gulped down a large mouthful of tea.

Obviously something was wrong. But what? Sarah broke off a piece of hot muffin and popped it in her mouth. It was horrible! Salty! Disgusting! Inedible!

"Oh, dear," said Olivia, trying not to laugh, "I think you put in twice the salt and half the sugar, Sara."

"I can't believe it!" howled Sara. "Can't I do anything right?"

Muriel patted Sara's hand. "Now, now, we all make mistakes. Don't we, Hetty?"

Hetty King stood in front of the class, appalled at the great uproar produced by the seventeen students of the one-room Avonlea Public School. Perhaps it was the fact that the Christmas break had given her ears a ten-day rest from the commotion, but it seemed to Hetty that the pre-school din had reached alarming proportions.

Muriel Stacey sat to one side of Hetty, looking rested and composed. She beckoned to Hetty and spoke in a mellow undertone.

"Hetty, please, don't you think it would be best if you and I discuss my announcement beforehand?"

"As I told you on the way here, Muriel," hissed Hetty emphatically, "school business is school business. Whatever announcement you have to make, I'm quite prepared to hear it at the same time as my students. We're already late as it is, so I suggest we simply proceed forthwith."

Muriel sighed.

Hetty straightened up and rapped the desk smartly. "Quietly! Quietly now! Class, please—please—" A mighty sneeze seized Hetty, much to the delight of the students.

"God bless you, Miss King," they intoned, in mock seriousness.

"Thank you," replied Hetty, blowing her nose vigorously. "Now please settle. Miss Stacey has an announcement to make." The din diminished to a few meagre scrapings and shufflings.

Muriel Stacey stood up and started to speak. Really, her honeyed tones would "calm a multitude," thought Sara.

"Class, as Superintendent of Schools, it is my job to ensure that Prince Edward Island excels in the world of education."

Hetty whipped her head sharply in Muriel's direction. "I think you'll find that my standards are comparable to—"

"To none, Miss King," said Muriel, soothingly, "to none. So, I'm sure that you will all be as pleased as I am that an idea I have long espoused has finally been approved by our rather old-fashioned Board of Education. I am pleased to announce that we are introducing, into the regular curriculum—Physical Education."

The effect these words had on the class was instant and electrifying. All the boys went wild, thumping their desks, whistling and generally showing their appreciation in the rowdiest ways possible. Sara felt a spasm of disappointment. Felicity and Cecily, too, looked unhappy. Of all the wonderful things they could have added to the curriculum— Greek, Latin, Romantic Poetry—they had chosen Physical Education! Rupert Gillis leapt onto his chair, unable to contain his excitement.

"Quiet down!" shouted Hetty. "Instantly! All of you! Rupert Gillis, get down off that chair this minute! Rupert, do as I say!"

Muriel Stacey's voice cut deftly through the din. "Your attention, please, class." The class fell immediately silent, and Muriel continued. "As the Board thinks it advisable that you take as much as possible of your exercise in the open air, we would encourage you to consider hockey as your winter sport."

Sara groaned, while the boys in the class responded with cheers. Hetty shook her head, clearly dismayed by Muriel's announcement.

Muriel smiled. "Our ladies' team in Charlottetown has had great success. I myself coach them, and do you know, they're so speedy they call themselves the Charlottetown Cannonballs!"

"Women!" brayed Rupert. "Playing hockey? I'd like to see that! Probably skate like you, Felix!"

Felix stood up, glaring, and proceeded to thump Rupert Gillis on the head with his geography textbook.

"Rupert! Felix! Stop that at once! I'll not speak to you again!" shouted Hetty. She was flushed with anger. None of this would be happening if Muriel hadn't made her ridiculous announcement!

"Of course," continued Muriel, "the class will have to select two captains, who in turn will select their teams."

Rupert's hand shot up. "Me! Me! I want to be a captain. And I think I should on account of how my Pa is coach of the Avonlea Avengers."

"That's only because he bought their sweaters, Gillis!," taunted Felix.

"You're just mad because you know you'll never be good enough to play for the Avengers! Never!"

"That's a dirty lie, Gillis," yowled Felix. "If I try out, I'll make the team, you just watch!"

Hetty spoke, an edge of sarcasm bordering her voice. "Clearly, you seem to have the matter in hand, Miss Stacey, so perhaps you should continue."

Muriel nodded. "Thank you. Now, of course this must be done democratically, so a show of hands, please, for Rupert Gillis as one of the team captains." Reluctantly, hands started to go up. Rupert had a reputation as a bully, and no one wanted to be the recipient of a well-placed punch in the schoolyard at the end of the day.

"You seem to have considerable support, Rupert, so you are elected as one of the captains," declared Muriel. "Now, do we have candidates for the second captain?"

"Andrew King!" hollered Felix.

"Andrew?" echoed Muriel.

"He's the best player in the school," announced Felix, emphatically. There were murmurs of agreement, a strong show of hands, and Andrew was elected as the opposing captain.

"We'll beat the pants off you!" threatened Rupert.

Andrew laughed. "I'd like to see you try!"

"Now, now," cautioned Muriel, "winning must take second place at all times to good sportsmanship.

Captains, you may take turns selecting your teams. Rupert, you go first, if you please."

"Fred Bell," grinned Rupert, and the desks soon emptied as the selected players lined up behind Rupert and Andrew.

Sara wanted to crawl away and die, just *die*! Everyone knew she couldn't skate, and she was small for her age, and she wasn't any good at pick-up soccer, or baseball, or any sport she had ever tried! She could feel a deep flush of shame spreading up her neck, working its way to her fair face. By the time it got there, she was the only one in the whole classroom left sitting. Frozen with humiliation, she didn't even look up when Felix spoke his hurtful words.

"Ha, ha, Rupert! Looks like you get Sara! Good luck!"

"You're the one who needs the luck, Felix King. What a bunch of weaklings. You ain't got a chance!"

Hetty rapped on the desk. "Silence!"

Muriel spoke softly. "Sara, as there seems to be an odd number of pupils in the class, perhaps I'll just assign you to Rupert's team. That way at least you'll be placed."

Sara stared down at the top of her desk.

"That's not fair!" protested Rupert. "She can't even skate!"

"Then I'm sure you'll be happy to give her a few pointers," directed Muriel. "Off you go now, Sara, over to Rupert's team."

Sara, feeling hot and ill, trudged over to stand at the end of Rupert's team. She hated hockey, she hated school, she hated everything! She just wanted to fall down and die from embarrassment. But that would have brought Sara even more unwanted attention, so she decided to go on living—at least until recess.

Chapter Seven

The horses trotted over the sparkling snow at a brisk clip, setting the sleighbells jingling. Usually Sara loved hopping in the sleigh and dashing along the road to town, but today she wished desperately that she had stayed home. The humiliation of being so clearly unwanted on the hockey team was bad enough, but now Sara was sandwiched between Hetty and Muriel, who were squabbling in a most unladylike manner.

"If you hadn't taken all that time selecting the hockey teams," snapped Hetty, "you wouldn't be in any danger of missing your train back to Charlottetown."

Muriel grabbed her hat as they careened around a curve in the road. Her elbow almost poked Sara in the eye, but she ducked just in time.

❧❧❧

"May hyenas dance on your mothers' graves
and may cherry stones jam your throats and choke you
three shades of purple, you brutes!
And you Archie Gillis..."

❧❧❧❧❧

Jasper Dale, who was trying out for goalie,
fell down as the puck winged by him.

❦❦❦

"Aunt Janet, what do you want me to do?
What can I do?"
"Just stay with me, Sara. I'll tell you what to do."

&

"Misfits! Misfits! Misfits!" chanted the crowd
as the final minutes of the hockey game
built to a frenzy.

"Hetty, you're exaggerating, as usual. I'm not going to miss my train!"

"I don't like pressing the horses when it's cold like this," replied Hetty, accusingly.

"Then slow down!" growled Muriel. "Hetty, what is going on? You really are in a beastly mood."

"I am not in a beastly mood," snarled Hetty. Since Hetty was already in a bad temper, Sara reasoned that her probing questions couldn't make the situation any worse.

"Does this have anything to do with John?" asked Sara, innocently.

Hetty reddened. "John who?"

"Your special friend from Halifax. You know, the boyfriend you brought to Avonlea all those years ago?"

"Why would this have anything to do with— John, or whatever his name was?"

Muriel gently interceded. "Hetty, don't you think Sara's old enough to know what happened? I truly think it would be so much better if we could talk about this. If you would just let me explain, I'm sure—"

"Explain what?" demanded Hetty. "That you stole a man who meant something to me? I don't think that bears much explaining, Muriel!"

"Hetty, I didn't steal him! After you left, he courted me, that's true, but—"

Hetty looked fierce. "Spare me the details, Muriel. I do not wish to talk about this matter any longer. The only matter I wish to address at the moment is the ridiculous Physical Education policy you are attempting to impose on my students! Competitive sports have no place in my school!"

As the two women batted the topic back and forth, Hetty's statement spun round and round in Sara's head. As Sara heard it, it was an even more passionate declaration than Hetty had perhaps intended "You stole the one man who ever meant something to me!" Sara had never heard Hetty speak that way about anything personal—it was incredible! Sara was determined to get to the bottom of it. But now wasn't the time to dig further.

"Nonsense, Hetty," replied Muriel. "The Greek ideal of education, the balance of spirit, mind *and* body, is what we're trying to achieve."

"We are living in Prince Edward Island," snipped Hetty, "not ancient Greece!"

Muriel took a deep breath as she prepared for the next volley. "Healthy bodies breed healthy minds. All the supervisors agree that the role of team sports in education is as important as—"

"Supervisors!" blasted Hetty. "Ha! Those who can't teach—supervise. I see no point in sacrificing my valuable class time to this, their latest, most ridiculous whim. These children get quite enough physical exercise, thank you, doing their chores."

"Chores do not promote team spirit and cooperation in quite the same way," countered Muriel, evenly.

Sara could see the main street of Avonlea come into view, and not a moment too soon. She was getting fed up with being in the middle of the argument, with Hetty and Muriel spitting at each other like two squirrels over one nut.

"Team spirit, my big toe!" snorted Hetty. "Competitive sports bring out the worst in people, not the best! I'll have no part in them."

There was a ringing silence as Muriel absorbed this. When she spoke again, it was in an eminently reasonable tone, the tone of one who knows she has the clinching argument on her side.

"Well, it's Board policy now, Hetty, so I'm afraid you'll have to cooperate. But, as one colleague to another, please, just try it. By the time I return, I'm sure you'll see the positive benefits of Physical Education in the curriculum as keenly as I do."

Hetty looked grim but said nothing more as they trotted down the main street towards the train station. Muriel reached across Sara and put her hand on Hetty's thin arm.

"I'm in good time to catch my train, Hetty, and I'd really like a bit of rock candy to fortify me on the journey back. Can we stop?"

Hetty checked the watch pinned to her coat, nodded and brought the team to a standstill outside Lawson's general store.

"Sara, aren't you coming in?" asked Muriel, as she stepped down from the sleigh.

Incredibly, even the thought of saltwater taffy and licorice sticks didn't interest Sara right now. She shook her head, and Muriel and Hetty entered Lawson's, leaving Sara to contemplate the new information about John and the romantic triangle. But no sooner had Sara started to fit the pieces together than Archie and Rupert Gillis came marching along, looking like men with a mission.

As Sara watched, Archie purposefully hammered up a cardboard sign on Lawson's, which announced in bold letters "MEN'S TRYOUTS FOR THE AVONLEA AVENGERS—SIGN UP HERE." He stood back, grinned and stood Rupert under the sign. Archie placed his large hand on top of Rupert's head, and drew a line two inches below. "Only men above this height need apply," he wrote below it.

"There, my boy, welcome to the Avonlea Avengers," Archie declared. Rupert beamed, and the two laughed, conspiratorially.

They're cheating! thought Sara. They're deliberately marking the line, just to make sure that Rupert gets a chance to try out for the team!

By now a small crowd had gathered, eager to sign up for the team. Archie picked three strapping lads to come to the tryouts at King Pond, and then Felix and Andrew came along. Felix excitedly jostled his way to the front of the crowd and presented himself to Archie Gillis.

Gillis smiled an oily smile. "Step right up, boy," he directed, moving Felix towards the mark on the wall. Felix was well below the black line. Archie shrugged. "Nice try, kid. Better come back in a few years."

Sara's anger spiked as she saw Felix flush with disappointment and frustration. Rupert grinned.

Sara sprang from the sleigh. "That's not fair, Archie Gillis! You drew that line—"

"So, you need a girl to defend you, Felix King!" sniggered Rupert.

"You porker, Gillis!" Felix bellowed as he lunged at Rupert, grabbing him around his waist.

Archie laughed. "Go to it, boys!"

"Felix, don't!" cried Sara.

"You little runt!" snarled Rupert, wrestling with Felix. Sara leapt on Rupert's back, which brought a great cheer from the crowd. Andrew joined the melee, trying to part the combatants.

"Felix, stop it! He'll make mincemeat of you!" he yelled.

The cheers and whistles of the crowd brought Hetty and Muriel running from the store. Hetty immediately took charge of the situation.

"Boys! Stop that brawling immediately, do you hear me? And Sara Stanley, come here at once!"

When Hetty spoke in that tone of voice, everyone, even Felix and Rupert, obeyed her. Andrew pried Felix loose, and the crowd became hushed. Sara, considerably subdued, joined Hetty.

"Chicken!" taunted Rupert, somewhat feebly.

"Just you wait, Gillis!" Felix muttered, as Andrew dragged him away.

"And you, Archie Gillis," lectured Hetty. "You ought to be ashamed of yourself, letting this happen."

"Boys will be boys, Miss King." Archie shrugged. "That's how they grow up."

"Nonsense! Sara, Felix, come along. Muriel, we have no further business here."

"Just a moment, Hetty, please." Muriel turned to Archie, fixing him with a disapproving glare. "Men only, Mr. Gillis? But the Avonlea Avengers have always been open to boys, as well."

"Look, Miss Macy, the—"

"It's Miss Stacey," corrected Muriel, as the crowd tittered.

"Well, look, Miss," Archie pressed on, "the Gillis Sawmill is proud to sponsor the Avonlea Avengers, and I'm proud to coach them. But there's no place on the ice for children. Hockey's a man's game!"

"But your own son is being allowed to try out, Mr. Gillis," protested Muriel. "That's hardly fair. And just look what it's led to."

"My Rupert's the size of a man, and I'll say what's fair on my team, Miss Stacey."

Hetty wheeled on Muriel. "You see the kind of attitude competitive sports evokes, Muriel? Dreadful business. Simply dreadful."

Muriel was about to respond when Peg Bowen popped up and jabbed her bony finger in Archie Gillis's chest.

"Men only!" she yawled. "You've got to be a man to recognize one, you yellow-bellied tree thief! I said it before and I'll say it again, a curse on you and your team, Archie Gillis!"

She fixed Archie with her smoldering eyes. Her voice dropped to a dark whisper.

"And how are Jeb and Zeke doing? Getting better, I hope."

With that, and a snorting laugh, Peg Bowen jammed her pipe in her mouth and strode off, with her three-legged dog limping to keep up.

"That was an accident, you—you shrew!" shouted Archie, red-faced.

"Crazy old woman," muttered Rupert, as the crowd started to drift away.

"I think we've had quite enough of this little drama," declared Hetty, taking Sara and Felix firmly in tow. "Muriel, you've a train to catch."

And sure enough, the long whistle of the steam engine echoed across the snowy hills as the 3:35 to Charlottetown chugged its way into Avonlea.

"But the Avengers haven't had an opening all season!" huffed Felix as they entered the sunny King kitchen. "I thought we'd actually have a chance to try out for the team."

"I don't see why you'd want to. I wouldn't play on Archie Gillis's team even if I could," spluttered Sara. "He's horrible!"

"It's easy for you to say," countered Felix. "You're nothin'. You don't even skate!"

Tears scalded the corners of Sara's eyes, and she looked away. Sometimes Felix could say hurtful things.

"Felicity, dear," suggested Janet, from the comfortable depths of her favorite chair, "perhaps Sara would like some cocoa?"

Felicity poured the thick, steaming chocolate into

Sara's waiting mug. "There you go, Sara," she said, kindly. "That should warm you up."

"And Felix, I think we've had enough talk about hockey for the moment. All I want to hear from you is a thank you to your Aunt Hetty for giving you a ride home from town," added Alec.

Felix sighed. "Thank you, Aunt Hetty."

"You're welcome, Felix. But you know, your father's quite right," Hetty added. "I was very upset to see people of our breeding, Kings, brawling on the main street this afternoon. It's disgraceful."

Sara sniffled. It just didn't make sense, people getting so upset about a game—just a game. But even as Sara was thinking this, she knew in her heart that she, too, was upset because of a game. Whatever the reasons, she felt incompetent and frustrated, just like Felix.

"Well, we mustn't linger," announced Hetty, briskly. "Olivia will be wondering where we've vanished to. No, no, Janet. Don't get up, dear, please—it's such an effort for you in your condition."

And it was true, Janet was immense now. However, she insisted on heaving her bulk from the chair. "There's something I want to give Sara," she gasped, red-faced from her exertions.

Felicity helped Janet to steady herself. "What is it, Mother? I'll get it."

"No, no, I want to," insisted Janet, as she started to move, with effort, towards the summer kitchen.

"Please, Aunt Janet," begged Sara, "let me help."

"No, thank you."

Alec sprang to Janet's side. "I'll get it, dear, I—"

"Stop it, all of you!" cried Janet. "I'm not an invalid! Stop treating me like one! I can't stand it!"

Sara was quite shocked at this outburst, since Aunt Janet was usually so good-natured and jolly. A silence fell on the group as Janet continued to work her way across the floor, disappearing into the summer kitchen.

"Oh, dear," murmured Hetty.

A worried look settled on Alec's face, and when he spoke, his voice was muted. "It's just so near her time. Dr. Blair said her moods are bound to be changeable."

"And they certainly are," added Felicity, quietly.

Janet emerged from the summer kitchen a moment later, carrying a pair of worn skates.

"Sara," she panted, "I want you to have these. Felicity's outgrown them, and they should fit you just fine."

Sara's heart sank. "It's very kind of you, Aunt Janet, but I think it's too late for me to learn how to skate."

"Nonsense! Anyone can learn. You just give it a try, Sara. After all, we don't want you left out of things."

"Now, Sara," prompted Hetty, "thank your Aunt Janet. After all, she went to a lot of trouble to get you those skates."

It was very confusing, thought Sara. On the one hand, she wanted to learn how to skate and play hockey and be part of the team, while, on the other, she just wanted to be Sara, telling stories and dreaming and not competing with anyone for anything. Hetty poked her.

"Thank you, Aunt Janet," said Sara. "This is very kind of you."

Janet fell back into the big chair with a grand thump. "You're welcome, dear," she puffed, as she fanned herself with her plump hand.

Chapter Eight

Sara whooped with dismay as, once again, her arms windmilled, her feet whirled out from under her and she went crashing to the ice. Gasping for air, perspiring inside her heavy red woollen coat, her mittens soaked with snow, Sara lay panting on her back, looking up at the brilliant winter sky. It just wasn't fair! Felicity and Cecily and even silly Sally Potts could all skate. Gliding gracefully across the ice, they looked like swans on a calm, summer river. I look like—like an elephant with a sprained knee! thought Sara. And that's when it's going well!

For the second morning in a row, Sara had risen at dawn, slipped out the back door, walked the short distance to the little pond at the bottom of the yard, strapped on her hand-me-down skates and proceeded to slide, tumble, crash and wobble across the ice. As a matter of fact, she did just about everything *except* skate. But Sara's pride wouldn't allow her to be coached, so this was the lonely task she had set herself. Whether she liked it or not, Sara told herself, she had to "grasp the nettle" and learn how to skate and compete, because that was the way the world worked.

Hetty watched from the kitchen window as Sara struggled to her feet, took one step forward, then another one, and another one, faster and faster, out of control—until she once again crashed to the ice. Hetty winced.

"Oh dear," murmured Olivia, as she joined Hetty at the window, "those are bruising falls. Poor Sara."

Hetty finished her cup of English breakfast tea. "That settles it," she announced, setting her teacup down with a clatter on the table.

"Settles what, Hetty?"

Hetty reached for her coat and muffler. "It," she confirmed, as she flung open the back door. "Sara?" She beckoned. "It's schooltime. Come along, now."

Sara waved weakly, crawled on her hands and knees to the edge of the ice and took off her skates, relieved that she had a reason to quit practicing.

As Hetty and Sara tramped to school, it ocurred to Sara that the sympathy brought on by her bruised knee might encourage Aunt Hetty to respond to some searching questions. As Sherlock Holmes once commented, "A good detective is always on the case!" But she'd have to proceed skilfully, deftly.

"Aunt Hetty, you look very nice today," Sara observed.

Hetty's eyebrows shot up. "I do? Good heavens, these are just everyday clothes, child. Nothing fancy. I'm not given to fancy things."

"Oh, I know. But I meant your—your face, Aunt Hetty. You must have been very pretty when you were young—younger I mean."

Hetty smiled. "Well, I had nice hair, if I do say so myself, and good posture. But I was no beauty, that's certain."

Sara limped as pathetically as she could. "A great poet once said 'Beauty is in the eye of the beholder,'" she mused, dreamily. "Your friend John must have thought you were beautiful, didn't he?"

Hetty paused. "Yes," she murmured, "I suppose he did."

Sara took a deep breath, choosing her next words carefully. "Aunt Hetty, when you said the other day that Miss Stacey had stolen him away, what did you mean?"

"Just that," snapped Hetty, breaking the mood like a string of beads. "John was my beau, and then he was Muriel's. There's nothing very mysterious about it. I'm sure it's a well-worn story. Now, that's all I'm going to say about it, Sara. It's a closed chapter. And I mean closed."

Hetty rapped her knuckles sharply on the desk. "Settle down class, now, please settle down. I have an announcement to make." Hetty's chin was set in a particularly determined manner. Even Rupert Gillis paid attention when Miss Hetty King looked that way. Hetty cleared her throat and spoke resolutely.

"I have made a decision regarding the introduction of hockey into the Avonlea curriculum." A wave of interest fanned through the class. Hetty continued.

"I have decided to follow my own deep beliefs in this matter. As of this announcement, the teams you selected will disband and hockey will not be played as part of our school program. That is all I have to say."

A shocked silence greeted this news. Holy Toledo! thought Sara. Aunt Hetty was disobeying Muriel Stacey, and the Provincial Board of Education, and the

government of the Dominion of Canada and probably—probably Aunt Hetty was even disobeying the
Queen of England! Sara looked up at the large framed
photograph of Queen Victoria, who gazed out over
the students of Avonlea with distant severity. I
wonder if *she* can skate? thought Sara. Well, queens
can do anything, so it was almost certain that if the
plump little monarch wanted to skate, she could!

"But Miss King, Miss King, I was elected captain," whined Rupert Gillis. "It ain't fair!"

Hetty looked unimpressed. "This is not a matter of
fairness, Rupert. This is a matter of principle. For those
of you who feel an overwhelming need to play hockey,
I suppose you can try out for the Avengers. But that is
no concern of mine. Now, please turn to your spellers.
I have nothing further to say on the matter."

"Are you absolutely sure, Miss King?" asked
Andrew, who was severely disappointed at not
having the opportunity to be captain of the team that
he was sure could beat any team of Rupert Gillis's.

Sara was terrifically relieved. She certainly
wouldn't miss her painful morning workouts on the
unforgiving pond, not to mention the almost certain
humiliation that would have befallen her when it
came time to actually play.

"That is my final word," confirmed Hetty.
"Now, let us review the new words we learned to

spell yesterday. And this one's tricky, class. Altogether, please, spell *embarrassment*. I repeat, *embarrassment*."

There was a great droning and muttering of many "r"s and far too many "s"s as the students of Avonlea School struggled to meet Hetty King's challenge.

Archie Gillis's shouted instructions sliced through the biting air as the would-be hockey players whizzed up and down the ice.

"Come on, men!" he hollered. "We've got a team to put together here! The Avonlea Avengers accept only the best, lads! Pass the puck through the middle there, Rupert!"

Archie clapped his beefy hands together, encouraging his son to skate harder and faster. Rupert took a mighty whack at the puck, but it careened off the wooden goalpost, lodging in one of the deep snowbanks ringing the pond. Jasper Dale, who was trying out for goalie, fell down as the puck winged by him. Poor Jasper! His skating skills were about as polished as his social skills. And if it were possible for someone to skate in a stammering fashion, then Jasper had achieved that dubious distinction.

As Archie angrily shouted Jasper off the ice, Malcolm MacGinty charged towards the snowbank, frantically dug out the puck with his stick and flipped it onto the ice. Once again, the players rocketed around the pond.

Felix looked miserable. "They kicked us off the ice so they could have their dumb tryouts," he lamented to Sara as they stood on the sidelines, watching the pick-up game.

"Archie Gillis still says we're too short," complained Andrew. Their recent confrontation with Archie in front of Lawson's store continued to rankle in the boys, and although Sara didn't think much of hockey as a game, she knew that Archie Gillis was being totally unfair.

"You know," urged Sara, "you've got to fight for something if you really, really want it."

Olivia nodded her agreement. Alec joined them, just in time to hear Sara's advice.

"Sara's right, boys. You can't just bellyache about the situation. You've got to stand on your own two feet if you want something badly enough. Go and ask Mr. Gillis to reconsider letting you try out for the Avengers. Go on, now. Give it a try."

Felix and Andrew looked at each other, nodded their agreement and took off, their blades flashing as they skated towards Archie, who was bellowing encouragement to the players. The boys snowplowed to a halt in front of the Avengers' coach.

Andrew took a deep breath. "Mr. Gillis? Mr Gillis, I realize that I may not be good enough to be on your team but—"

"He is so!" interrupted Felix, defiantly. "He's the best player in the school!"

Archie was concentrating on the action on the ice and seemed scarcely to hear the boys' entreaties. Andrew pressed on.

"What I'm trying to say is, could I at least have the chance to try out?"

"Couldn't we *all* have a chance to try out?" added Felix, his plump face flushed with concern.

Archie shifted the matchstick he was chewing from one side of his mouth to the other. "You taller than the mark?"

"No, sir," replied Andrew, "but—"

"Then I already told you, you can't try out. You know the rules."

"But it ain't fair!" wailed Felix. "You made the mark just shorter than Rupert, Mr. Gillis. Sara Stanley saw you do it!"

Archie shrugged. "Rules are rules."

Alec and Sara, who could see from a distance that the boys weren't making any headway in their case, joined them. Alec took up the boys' cause.

"Archie, surely you could give the boys a break. They're really quite good, you know. But even if you turned them down, at least they'd feel that they had a fair chance. What do you say?"

Archie glared at Alec. "What do I say? I'll tell you what I say, Alec King. Just because you used to play for the Avengers doesn't make you a coach. And it doesn't mean I have to do you and your little runts any favors, either. Now get out of here, I've got a team to put together."

"We aren't runts!" protested Sara, who was always a bit sensitive about her height.

"Come on, Sara," said Alec, "come on, boys. We're dealing with a hopeless case here."

"You're the hopeless one, King!" spluttered Archie. He spread his arms to take in all the players on the pond and raised his voice. "The whole bunch of you—you can't skate, you can't pass, you're not worthy of the name Avengers! You're—"

Archie Gillis stopped in mid-sentence. And what caused him to stop was a stranger who had glided onto the ice with compelling grace and speed. He was thoroughly bundled up against the cold. A long, blue scarf coiled round his neck met his bushy mustache, while a pulled-down woollen toque grazed the top of his thick spectacles.

"You there!" called Archie. "You here for the tryouts?"

The stranger nodded and deftly maneuvered his hockey stick as he streaked by.

Archie grinned. "Well, don't waste my time, man. Get out there and show me what you can do!"

The stranger skated brilliantly, weaving in and out of the players, easily scoring a goal and then easily scoring another one. Everyone immediately sensed that this man had special gifts when it came to playing hockey. It wasn't just what he did, thought Sara, but what he didn't do. He didn't waste a movement; he didn't shout or violently bodycheck. He went where the puck was going, not where it had been. In short, he was amazing. But who on earth was he?

Archie Gillis was beaming. "Now, that fella's a real hockey player! We've got our star, I just know it."

Archie blew his whistle and the action stopped. The tryout players took a much-needed break and skated off the ice, panting. Archie lifted his voice, calling to the stranger.

"Come over here! I've got a place for you and no two ways about it!"

The man sailed over to the group and stopped. He looked down, modestly.

"You want me on your team?" he muttered.

"You bet your blades I want you on my team!" exclaimed Archie. "You can skate, you can pass, and most of all—you can score!"

The stranger looked up, a defiant curl to his mustache. Then, as the startled group watched, he pulled off his toque, his mustache and his thick spectacles. There, revealed for everyone to see, was Peg Bowen!

Sara gasped. Archie Gillis's jaw dropped. Peg's coal-black eyes glinted in the winter sunshine. She shook out her thick, wiry hair.

"So, you want me on your team, do you, Archie Gillis?" She laughed spitefully. "I thought you said hockey was a man's game! No place for children—or women! You're not only a destroyer of nature, you're a bloody hypocrite!"

Sara thought Peg looked magnificent as she stared Archie down. Archie's jaw flapped, and people nearby started to laugh.

Sara grinned. "Somebody could put together a pretty good hockey team from all the people you've eliminated, Mr. Gillis."

Alec laughed. "Sara's right, Gillis. I don't think you have the keenest eye for talent."

Archie flushed. "Then why don't *you* go ahead and pick a team, Alec King? That way you can have all the misfits you want on it!"

Alec's face grew dark. "I wouldn't call the boys who happen to be a quarter of an inch shorter than some arbitrary mark on a poster 'misfits.'"

"I don't care what you call them. Go ahead! Start you own team, if you've got the nerve," challenged Archie.

"Come on, Pa," enthused Felix, "we can do it! Honest we can!"

"We'll show them, Uncle Alec," chorused Andrew.

Alec paused a moment, deciding. "All right, Gillis. I will. You're on. I'll be proud to coach a team called the Misfits!"

Peg fixed Archie with a penetrating look. "So, Archie Gillis, are you absolutely sure the Avengers will beat us?"

"Dead sure."

Peg smiled, a little. "Well, maybe you'd like to make a bet with me. If the Misfits win, will you promise to honor the previous cutting limits around Avonlea and leave the forests in peace?"

Archie snorted. "And when *I* win?"

"Then you can cut anywhere you please," replied Peg, quietly.

Archie stuck out his sizable hand. "It's a bet," he said, as Peg applied her strong grip.

"All right," confirmed Alec, "name a date."

"A week tomorrow," suggested Archie. "Or do you need longer?"

"A week tomorrow is fine."

Sara grinned. "You'd better get back to work, Mr. Gillis. You've got to find someone to replace Mr. Peg Bowen!"

Chapter Nine

"Thank you, Hetty, that was the most delicious apple crumble, really quite scrumptious," purred Muriel Stacey as she spooned up the last of the dessert.

"Thank you," replied Hetty, a little aloof. "Olivia prepared it."

"Oh, could I have the recipe, Olivia? I would treasure it, I assure you."

Olivia smiled her thanks. "Of course, Muriel. I'll jot it down for you."

Hetty pushed her chair back from the table. "Well, I can't dilly-dally here. I've grammar tests to mark. Sara, if you would clear away the dessert dishes, please?"

Sara sighed and nodded. This morning Muriel Stacey had arrived for another stay at Rose Cottage. She planned to inspect the schools at nearby Markdale and Park Corners, and although she would be gone during the days, she would be, as Hetty put it, "in her hair" during the evenings. It was interesting, thought Sara. She herself was getting to like Muriel more and more. Muriel was really very little trouble, as houseguests go, always ready to help and smooth the way. The odd thing was that Sara could almost feel Aunt Hetty trying *not* to be friends with Muriel Stacey, even though she wanted to. It was as though Hetty had the opportunity to take a lovely tramp through the woods but deliberately set brambles and bushes and clusters of nettles in her own path. If only the two could talk it out, things would be so much better!

"Hetty, before you go," said Muriel, "I was wondering if you could share with me what progress you've made on the new policy on Physical Education?"

"I see. You've come to spy on me, have you?"

Olivia reddened. "Hetty, really, Muriel is only asking a question that is well within her rights to ask. I think you're over reacting just a bit, don't you?"

Hetty sucked her cheeks in, pulling her mouth into a prune. "This is school business, Olivia, and I would appreciate you holding your tongue."

Olivia looked away and offered nothing further.

Really! thought Sara. Aunt Hetty was being completely unreasonable. And it was ridiculous, because Muriel was going to discover the truth one way or another. Besides, Sara happened to think that her Aunt Hetty was right. Sports brought nothing but grief!

"Miss Stacey," Sara piped up, "Aunt Hetty has disbanded the school hockey teams. She feels that academic subjects are more important and, to tell you the truth, I'm relieved. My spelling is a lot better than my skating!"

Hetty shot Sara a withering look. Sara withered. Muriel addressed Hetty directly, speaking in a reasonable tone.

"Is this true, Hetty? Have you disbanded the hockey teams?"

"Yes, it's true," concurred Hetty, starchily. "You can report to the Board in Charlottetown that *no* progress has been made at the Avonlea School as far as intramural sports are concerned. And if I am allowed to continue my classes in my own fashion, as I have successfully done for the past twenty-odd years, I assure you there will be no progress made in the future, either!"

But Muriel Stacey was not a woman who was easily intimidated, and she'd known Hetty a long time.

"My, my," mused Muriel, sipping her tea, "I'm rather surprised to hear that. I'm told that you and your family have become quite involved in competitive sports."

Hetty sniffed. "What do you mean?"

"I understand your brother, Alec, is coaching a new hockey team to take on the Avengers. They're even placing bets on the game, I've heard. Quite a to-do, it seems. I had hoped that you'd had a change of heart."

Hetty turned pink. "That—that is my brother's doing, not mine. Some of my family can be quite disloyal, it seems. No, no. There will be no change of heart on my part, Muriel Stacey. You can count on that. Now, if you'll excuse me, I have papers to mark!"

With that, Hetty strode from the dining room and up the stairs, where the purposeful closing of her bedroom door punctuated the end of the discussion.

"Oh, dear," groaned Sara. "I shouldn't have said anything, I just shouldn't have. Now Hetty thinks I'm disloyal!"

Muriel patted Sara's hand. "Now, now, Sara, I had already heard about Hetty's actions. I just wanted her to confirm them herself."

"You didn't do anything wrong, dear," added Olivia, in her tender way.

Hetty's footsteps sounded on the stairs as she descended to the hall.

"Hetty?" called Olivia. "Is something wrong?"

Hetty popped her head in the door. Her warmest hat was jammed on her head and, clearly, she was about to go out.

"I'm going for a walk. I think the fresh air will do me good. And you three seem to be having a fine time without me."

"Oh, Hetty," sighed Muriel. "You're being far too sensitive."

Hetty nodded brusquely. "I'll be back in an hour or so."

"Aunt Hetty," begged Sara, "please let me come with you, please?"

Hetty looked at Sara and was struck by how much she looked like Ruth—the same passion, the same intensity—her dear, dear sister Ruth, whose death had nearly broken Hetty's heart.

"Yes, Sara," Hetty said, her voice softening, "if you want to come, why, yes, that would be fine. But mind you bundle up now, it's a cold evening."

Sara sprang up from the table and sprinted to the hall, hugging Hetty as she skidded by. "Oh, thank you, Aunt Hetty. I'll bundle up, don't you worry."

Hetty smiled at Muriel, almost apologetically. "Sara's a very emotional child, she feels things very keenly."

"As do you, Hetty," replied Muriel, "as do you."

Janet King smiled her thanks as Alec added a fresh log to the fire that warmed the snug parlor of the King farm. Felicity, Felix and Cecily were all in bed, and it was that time of evening when parents become couples again, companionable and relaxed.

As Janet watched the orange flames dance to their silent, ancient music, a tiny leg jammed up against her ribcage. Janet shifted in her chair, stretching to give the wee creature inside her room to move. The baby had a schedule of its own as it grew in the warm, liquid twilight of Janet's body. It had periods of sleep, periods of slight movement and—as right now—periods of intense activity. Really, thought Janet, this little one was going to be a runner—or a hockey player!

Alec handed Janet a cup of thick, steaming cocoa and sat down on the chair beside her. He said nothing, which signaled to Janet that he definitely had something on his mind.

"Alec, do you have something to tell me?"

Alec lifted an eyebrow. "Who? Me?"

"Really, Alec, you don't live with someone for fifteen years and not know such things. Now, by any chance does it involve coaching a hockey team to take on the Avonlea Avengers?"

"Well," Alec confessed, "there is a little game planned."

"A little game?"

"All right, a big game."

"When?" inquired Janet.

"Next week."

"Next week!" shrieked Janet. "Alec, I could be in labor next week!"

Alec smiled a bit sheepishly. "I know, dear. But I'll make sure I'm here—you can count on it."

"Who's on this team of yours?" Janet growled.

"Uh—well, yes, Felix and Andrew and Freddy Bell and—"

"Alec, those are children!" Janet interrupted, shaking her head in dismay. "You can't just make a team up of children and pit them against Archie Gillis and his hulks. Good Lord, Felix would be flattened by some of those players!"

"It's not all children," countered Alec. "Jasper's on the team, and—"

"Jasper?" echoed Janet, incredulously. "Alec, you're going to be trounced!"

Alec reached for his most reasonable tone. "Now, now, Janet, what we lack in experience we'll make up for in heart. Besides, Peg Bowen is going to be a great help."

Janet's jaw dropped. "Peg? Bowen?" she croaked.

"Oh, yes," declared Alec, "she's a tremendous hockey player, quite brilliant, in fact."

"Really, Alec," exclaimed Janet, "what a bunch of misfits!"

Alec smiled wryly. "Well, actually, dear, that's what we're calling ourselves—the Avonlea Misfits."

"Oh, Alec, it's just that Dr. Blair said I'm close to my time, and you're going to be involved with this hockey thing, and..." Tears sprang to Janet's eyes. She hated this, being ambushed by emotion.

Alec took her hand and spoke warmly but resolutely. "Now you listen to me, Janet King. I am going to be here when the baby's born and that's a promise no one and nothing will make me break."

Janet's soft snuffling was interrupted by a loud knock on the front door. Alec didn't move. Janet smiled weakly.

"You'd better go and see who it is, dear—"

Just then, Hetty sailed into the parlor, with Sara in tow. Hetty stood, feet apart, like a great admiral on the prow of a mighty ship in the middle of a naval battle. She fired.

"Alec King, how dare you put us in the position of having to defend the honor of the King family name by getting involved in a ridiculous hockey match!"

Alec ducked. "Now, slow down, Hetty. What do you mean 'the King family name'?"

"You accepted that nonsensical challenge from Archie Gillis. Everyone knows it, and now you—and I and all the Kings—are the laughingstock of the town. How could you?"

Alec fired back. "There's a lot more at stake than the King name, Hetty. You know perfectly well what Archie Gillis is up to. If he isn't stopped, there won't be a tree left in Avonlea!"

"The trees!" sniped Hetty. "Sara explained to me about Peg Bowen's foolish bet. She must be crazier than we thought!"

It's funny, thought Sara, for someone who didn't believe in competitive sports, Aunt Hetty could be pretty darn competitive!

Janet lifted herself from the chair. "Hetty! Alec!" she hissed. "Keep your voices down! You'll wake the children. And it's hardly suitable for Sara to hear such arguing between brother and sister."

"I don't mind," chirped Sara. "It's really quite interesting."

"Competitive sports," growled Hetty. "It's not enough that I have Muriel Stacey breathing down my neck in my own classroom, promoting the most uncivilized behavior I have ever witnessed. Now I have to face it amongst my own kin!"

Janet was quite red in the face. "Hetty, no one in this house has ever put the King name to shame. And besides, I think Alec will make a wonderful coach. He can do anything he sets his mind to. So there!" She collapsed into the chair, breathing heavily. Alec grinned at her. She was still his wonderful, loyal Janet—the girl he had married.

Hetty paused as she prepared her final volley. "I might have known I couldn't count on you to talk sense to him, Janet. Alec, I warn you, whatever team you've put together, it had better be a darn good one because—trees, or no trees—the very reputation of our family depends on it!"

"All I need is a couple of strong skaters," countered Alec.

"What you need," announced Hetty, "is a miracle."

"Uncle Alec," begged Sara, "please, can I be on the team? I've been practicing hard! And I want to do my part to uphold the King name, oh, please?"

"Sara!" barked Hetty, "you are not going to involve yourself in this—this unseemly contest. I won't hear of it."

"But Aunt Hetty, aren't I part of the King family? You just said, the very reputation of the family depends on who wins the game. Well, I want to help out. Uncle Alec, what do you say?"

Alec shook his head. "Sara, I can't throw you out on the ice with the Avengers. They play a rugged game, and besides, I've already selected our team. I hope you understand."

Tears tickled the corners of Sara's eyes. She didn't want to understand! She wanted to help! Was she part of the family or not?!

Janet gently touched Sara's shoulder, and spoke quietly to Alec.

"Alec, dear, couldn't Sara be a sub? You know, if anyone gets injured or too tired to play, Sara could fill in, if only for a few minutes."

"Well, I suppose—"

"Oh, thank you, Uncle Alec." Sara's face broke into a grin. "You won't be sorry, I promise you. I'm going to practice and practice!"

"I don't approve of this, Alec," snapped Hetty.

"I know you don't, Hetty," Alec snapped back, "but I'm the coach of the Misfits, not you."

"Well, I never..." sniffed Hetty.

"Exactly," said Alec. "Exactly."

Chapter Ten

A rosy, early-morning sun glowed low in the milky-blue sky as Sara strapped on her skates and skated onto the glinting ice of the small pond behind Rose Cottage. The air was perfectly still, and the only sounds were the faint roar of the ocean in the distance and the sizzle of Sara's blades as they slashed the ice. One thing Sara had learned was that if you felt yourself falling, it was usually better to lean forward than to lean back. Usually. But not always. Which is why, after two turns around the pond, Sara found herself sprawled, face down, on the frozen surface.

"Oh no," she wailed, "I'll never learn, never!"

"Never say never, Sara." Muriel Stacey's smooth tones snowed down on Sara, who squinted up at her.

"Miss Stacey! I thought you'd left for Markdale."

Muriel pulled a grateful Sara to her feet. "I don't have to leave for half an hour. And since Hetty seems determined to do the breakfast dishes on her own, I thought I'd put on my skates and give you a hand. After all, I do coach my own girls' team in Charlottetown. Will you accept my help, Sara? What do you think?"

"I think I need all the help I can get," moaned Sara.

So Muriel guided Sara around the pond, advising her to glide and not walk, and giving her pointers on how to keep her balance. Muriel herself was a wonderful skater, and when she turned to skate backwards, she gripped Sara's hands and pulled her along at an exhilarating speed. And so it was that Sara found herself face to face with Muriel Stacey, and questions that had been bubbling in Sara's mind popped to the surface.

Sara swallowed nervously. "Miss Stacey, I was wondering if you could help me out with something I'm trying to investigate."

"I'll certainly try," replied Muriel, as they whirled around a corner.

"When Aunt Hetty said the other day that you stole her boyfriend away, what did she mean exactly?"

Muriel paused. "Did you ask your Aunt Hetty about this, Sara?"

"Yes," replied Sara. "But she said it was a closed chapter."

"Perhaps she's right," cautioned Muriel.

"I'm not an infant, Miss Stacey," countered Sara, "and it is part of my family history, in a way."

Muriel considered this. "I suppose it is—in a way. But this must be kept between us, Sara."

Sara nodded vigorously.

"Well, after Hetty came back to Avonlea to teach, John and I got engaged to be married."

"Engaged!" gasped Sara.

"It didn't work out, for reasons which I won't go into. But Hetty wasn't the only one who suffered pain, I can assure you."

"But you were her friend!" accused Sara. "How could you do that?!"

"Everyone makes choices, Sara. Hetty had rejected John, very clearly. We weren't traitors, although Hetty thinks we were. At any rate, my girl, that's all I have to say about the matter. Anything else you'll have to find out from Hetty. Now, once more around the pond, and then I must be on my way. Head up, now, Sara, head up—oh, dear!!"

This time both Muriel and Sara went tumbling to the ice in a tangled heap of arms and legs and skates and skirts. By the time they got sorted out, Muriel was late for Markdale and Sara had to run to school, puffing and panting in the cold air, with thoughts of John and Miss Stacey and Aunt Hetty bouncing up and down in her mind. But a busy school day, with much chatter about the hockey game, and the bets being laid, and the whole town turning out for the game, pushed these thoughts to the back of Sara's mind. And that's where they were when Sara arrived at the King farm pond, after school, for hockey practice.

The Misfits swarmed around the rink like wasps drawn to spilt lemonade at a summer picnic. Jasper Dale wasn't swarming, however. He stood in the goal crease, hovering in an unreassuring fashion. Sara, too, wobbled uncertainly on the ice as Peg Bowen and Felix and Andrew streaked by her, shouting for the puck. Alec watched from the sidelines, shouting instructions, trying to whip his team into some kind of shape. Felix came flying past Sara, chasing the puck.

"I've got! I've got it!" he hollered. "Get out of my way, Sara!!"

Sara swayed and fell as Felix rocketed by.

"Felix! That's enough!" roared Alec. "No more of that!"

Felix carved a full turn and came back to Sara. "Pa just let you on the team because he felt sorry for you," he razzed. "You can't even skate, for crying out loud."

Sara struggled to her feet. "That's not true, Felix King!" But in her heart, Sara felt otherwise. Look at me, she thought, I can't even get around the rink, much less pass or score. I'm hopeless!

"It's good luck that you're just a sub," stated Felix. "That means you'll never get to play."

Peg Bowen whizzed up, looking particularly fierce. "Leave her alone, Felix. She's on our team now."

"You can't boss me around," growled Felix. "My Pa's the coach, not you."

Sara couldn't bear any more of this and staggered towards the edge of the rink.

"You were doing fine, Sara," said Alec, encouragingly.

"It's no use," Sara announced. "They don't want me on their team." She plunked down in the snow and started taking her skates off.

"Sara, don't pay any attention to them!"

Sara felt hot and tearful, and she just wanted to escape from the whole ghastly situation. She tugged at her skates.

Alec watched her, helpless. "Well, at least go up to your Aunt Janet and get a cup of cocoa, Sara," he suggested, kindly. "You'll feel better later, I'm sure of it."

Sara said nothing more as she trudged away from the pond towards the farmhouse, tears scalding her eyes.

Alec turned his attention back to the practice. He clapped the players to a halt, and they gathered in front of him.

"All right, everyone, let's get off our high horses here, shall we? I want to win this game as much as you do, but the important thing is that we play as a team and have a good time." He looped a look at Felix. "I don't want arguments and nastiness. I want us to enjoy the game, and for that, we've got to pull together. Now, are you with me?"

"Yes, sir!" they all shouted. Everyone except Jasper Dale, who, without the support of the net, toppled to the ice.

Alec sighed. "Jasper, are you all right?"

Jasper fumbled to retrieve his hat, which had skittered away in sprightly fashion. "Y-yes," he stammered. "H-h-hat..."

"Good. Now let's keep sharpening our defense. The game's tomorrow. Off you go then! Rally, rally, rally!" thundered Alec.

As the players raced down the ice, shooting the puck back and forth, Alec skated backwards, intent on the play. The next thing he knew, he was looking up at his whole team, who were crowded around him with anxious looks on their faces. Alec tried to move but inhaled sharply as a searing pain shot through his body.

Peg Bowen crouched down and fixed him with her dark eyes. "Well, Coach, I think you've sprained your back. The next move for you is up to the house." Alec moaned. "Easy, boys," advised Peg, "we'll have to carry him."

Sara, shivering, knocked with a mittened hand on the kitchen door of the King farmhouse and waited for a reply. There wasn't one, so she pushed the door open and entered the large, bright kitchen. As she dropped her skates on the floor and started to strip off her wet coat, she became aware of muted sounds nearby.

"Aunt Janet?" she called softly as she walked into the living room. "Is that you?"

Janet hastily wiped her eyes before turning to Sara. Janet was very tired and dispirited, but she didn't want to frighten Sara by revealing her precarious emotional state. She forced a smile.

"Oh, Sara. I didn't hear you come in."

"Aunt Janet, I've brought the skates back," Sara informed her glumly. "Thanks for lending them to me."

"But they're yours to keep, dear."

"I don't want to skate. There's no point."

"Now, now," comforted Janet, taking Sara's hand, "that's not the spirit I'm used to seeing in you."

"They don't want me on the team anyway. They're all being so horrible and I feel like a fool, standing like a lump of clay while they whiz around."

"Well, you just can't listen to what everyone says, Sara," counseled Janet. "If you did, you wouldn't know whether you were coming or going. You've got to believe in yourself, dear."

"Oh, Aunt Janet, I'm not confident like you!" Sara wailed.

Sara's words pierced Janet's fragile mood and, once again, she found herself in tears. Snuffling and gasping, she groped in her apron for a handkerchief. Sara, alarmed, leapt to her side.

"Aunt Janet! What's wrong?"

Janet smiled feebly. "Oh, I'm a fine one to be giving advice. I don't have a confident bone in my body. Sara, I'm so worried."

"About what?" asked Sara, earnestly.

"Everything," wailed Janet. "I haven't given birth in ten years. I'm so scared!"

Now it was Sara's turn to take Janet's hand. "You'll be fine, Aunt Janet, I'm sure of it."

Janet looked unconvinced. "Taking care of an infant again—I think I've forgotten how."

"Of course you haven't!" exclaimed Sara.

Janet dabbed at her eyes. "I can barely take care of the three I have now."

"Don't be silly," replied Sara, "you're a wonderful mother."

Janet brightened a bit. "Do you really think so?"

"Of course. You're the best. And you'll have lots of help. Uncle Alec is a wonderful father, and Felicity is dying to lend a hand with the baby. You'll be just fine, you'll see."

Janet struggled out of the chair and gave Sara a big hug. It was the strangest hug Sara had ever received, because she was plastered right up against Janet's very large, very firm, belly. Sara felt as though she were hugging two people, not one, which was really the case, when you thought about it.

Janet's voice was suffused with warmth. "Thank you, Sara. You've no idea how I needed to hear those things." She blew her nose energetically. "But enough of this. You and I are going to stop feeling sorry for ourselves. Let's make a bargain, shall we? If I stop moaning about my situation, you'll take another run at skating. What do you say?"

Sara looked up at Janet and nodded. "I say it's a deal."

"Good," said Janet, moving towards the kitchen. "Then let's get back to the pond."

Suddenly, Felix burst through the kitchen door, bellowing like a walrus with a headache.

"Ma! Ma! Come quick! Father's sprained his back or somethin'!"

Janet's hand sprang to her throat. "Good Lord," she whispered.

"What happened, Felix?" demanded Sara.

"Here he is now!" trumpeted Felix, as Peg and Jasper carried Alec into the house. Janet looked down at him—the wounded warrior home from battle.

"Oh, Alec," she croaked.

Alec looked up, trying to smile through the haze of pain. "Hello, dear. I—I'm home early."

"But Hetty," confirmed Olivia, "Dr. Blair says Alec could be laid up for weeks!"

Sara reached for another gingersnap.

"Just one more cookie, Sara, supper isn't that far off," warned Hetty, as she stirred a rich, fragrant stew bubbling on the kitchen stove. Sara bit into the delicious cookie. A few crumbs sprayed to the floor, where Topsy licked them up in a flash.

"Don't worry, Aunt Hetty," advised Sara. "Uncle Alec just needs bed rest. He'll be fine—eventually."

"How will that help us?" growled Hetty. "The game's tomorrow."

Olivia looked amazed. "You mean you still want this ridiculous game to be played?"

"Olivia, have you completely lost your senses?" barked Hetty. "Of course the blasted game still has to be played. We'll be the laughingstock of the entire village if it isn't."

"But without a coach, I just don't see how it's possible," countered Olivia.

"Well, we'll just have to put our thinking caps on," instructed Hetty. "We'll have to find a new coach, and quick about it."

An idea flashed across Sara's mind, like a trout in a pond. Yes! The perfect solution!

"Aunt Hetty, I have a suggestion. And a very good one, if I say so myself."

"Well, what is it, child? Spit it out."

"I know just the person to ask," suggested Sara, gravely. "This person has all kinds of experience coaching hockey and is *very* committed to team sports."

Hetty raised a sharp eyebrow. "I'm waiting, Sara."

"Muriel Stacey!" declared Sara. "That's who can coach the Misfits. And she's right upstairs. It's perfect, Aunt Hetty! All you have to do is go up and ask her."

"Are you out of your mind?" cried Hetty. "I will not ask Muriel to help me out. Absolutely not!"

"I think Sara's suggestion is an excellent one, Hetty," echoed Olivia. "When you think about it, it really makes a lot of sense."

"And you did say that her team has done awfully well in Charlottetown," Sara reminded Hetty.

"Hummph," muttered Hetty, peering into the stew pot.

Sara felt daring. "Or won't you ask Muriel because she was engaged to John, and you've never forgiven her for it?" she asked.

Hetty's jaw dropped, as much as a lady's jaw should. "Sara Stanley!"

Sara pressed on. "Even though you refused him yourself? I mean, John did ask you to marry him, didn't he?"

Hetty's eyes narrowed. "I can only think of one person who would be so indiscreet as to tell you such things!"

"Oh, Aunt Hetty," pleaded Sara, "can't you forget what's past and find forgiveness in your heart? I think Miss Stacey would be a true friend to you, if you'd just let her explain."

Hetty's face was clouded as she stirred the supper stew with alarming speed.

"I will not beg Muriel Stacey for any favors and that's the end of it. The *end*!"

Chapter Eleven

Hetty spent a restless night, dream-tossed and sleep-wrecked. She knew Sara's suggestion to ask Muriel to coach the Misfits was a good one, but she simply couldn't swallow her pride and raise the matter. However, in the early morning, when she saw Sara once again struggling with her skates and a battered hockey stick on the back pond, Hetty knew that she must ask for help. She poured a cup of hot tea, patted her hair and knocked on Muriel's bedroom door.

As Muriel opened the door, the delicate scent of English powder wafted out into the hall. In the morning light she looked quite handsome, her strong features softened by the color of the robe she was wearing—a most becoming shade of rose.

"How very kind of you, Hetty," Muriel said. "Won't you come in?"

Hetty forced a smile. "Well—I suppose so."

Muriel sipped the tea. "Delicious!" she declared. "Hetty, do you remember when we roomed together at teachers' college, how old Miss Binsley would make us drink that dreadful beef tea of hers when we got sick?" Muriel chuckled. "What was it we used to say? 'Binsley's tea would—would—'"

"'Would sting a bee,'" finished Hetty.

"Oh, Hetty, what good times we had."

Hetty looked out the window. "Well, that was a long time ago," she mumbled, her voice embroidered with a small, sad edge.

"It's never too late to mend a friendship, Hetty," Muriel offered.

Hetty paused. "Muriel, I—"

"Yes?" prompted Muriel, hopeful that Hetty was going to bend and at least discuss their rift.

"I—that is, we—we're in a bit of a bind and—"

"We certainly are," agreed Muriel.

"I mean, the hockey team—the Misfits. Well, I was wondering if..." Hetty took a deep breath, and struggled on. "Muriel, I was—wondering if we could call on you—to do us the favor of, well—of helping out."

Muriel shook her head. So that's what this visit was all about!

"I don't see how that's possible, Hetty. I'm scheduled to return to Charlottetown tomorrow morning."

Hetty looked grim. "Please, please, Muriel. For the sake of the King name. I mean, I mean—for the sake of the team."

"I'm sorry, I don't see—"

Hetty was desperate. "Well, then for the sake of the—the trees! Couldn't you help us? Please?"

Muriel paused while she decided. "Very well, Hetty. I will stay and take Alec's place as coach—"

Hetty exploded with relief. "Oh, thank you!"

"—on one condition," cautioned Muriel. "You must institute an intramural sports program in your school."

"Well, I hardly think that the one has anything to do with the other," argued Hetty.

"Then in that case, Hetty, I'm sorry. We really have nothing further to discuss."

Hetty flushed. "Very well! It's a bargain. *If*, but only if, the Misfits win."

"I think that's a safe wager," Muriel assured her. "You see, I have a little card up my sleeve just waiting to be played."

The day of the hockey match between the Avengers and the Misfits dawned as clear and crisp as one of Hetty's arithmetic lessons. But it wasn't a school day, thought Sara, as she tumbled out of bed, it was a Saturday. The Saturday of The Big Game!

Sara scrambled into her clothes and ran down to the pond for a final practice. She was definitely skating more competently, and yesterday, at hockey practice, she had actually managed to score a goal! This miracle had occurred because Peg Bowen gave her an important piece of advice—a piece of advice Peg called "Right Place, Right Time."

"Don't you worry about skating, Sara," Peg had whispered. "Just position yourself in front of the goal and wait for a pass. That way you'll be in the Right Place at the Right Time."

And sure enough, Peg had passed to Sara, who was standing sentry-like by the goal, and Sara had fired into the net and—lo and behold—she made the score! Maybe, just maybe, she would score a goal today—a goal that would win The Big Game for the Misfits! If that happened, the cheering would be monumental, and Sara would be a local hero. She would be carried around the ice on the team's shoulders and everyone in town would be watching and cheering, and Aunt Olivia would write up the story for the Avonlea *Chronicle* and—

"Sara! Sara!" shouted Hetty from the back door. "Breakfast is ready! Come along, now, we mustn't be late!"

And so it was that Sara's dreams of glory faded into the contemplation of a large bowl of oatmeal porridge laced with Jamaican molasses. Really, Sara sighed, porridge was hardly the Food of the Conquering

Hero! Or rather, Heroine. But it was, as Hetty remarked, "fortifying."

The usual Saturday activities of Avonlea—shopping, picking up mail and gossiping outside Lawson's store—had been laid aside as folks gathered, excited, at the King pond for The Big Game. Well, actually, the gossiping hadn't been laid aside. In fact, it took centre stage as people traded information and discreetly laid wagers on the outcome of the game. The betting was running heavily in favor of Archie Gillis's team, and little wonder, for the Avengers looked sleek and menacing as they sprinted around the ice, expertly passing the puck back and forth. The Misfits observed warily from the sidelines, catching their breath after their own somewhat haphazard practice session.

Archie Gillis swaggered up to Hetty and Muriel, who were standing with Janet and Olivia watching the Avengers as they streaked up and down the pond. He gazed down at the women.

"I was so sad to hear about Alec's little accident," he offered insincerely. "Why don't you just concede defeat right now, ladies? It will save us all a bit of grief."

"Oh, hardly, Mr. Gillis," replied Janet, brightly. "That isn't what my husband wants at all, let me assure you."

"It's you who should concede defeat, Mr. Gillis," suggested Hetty, stiffly. "I believe you know Miss Muriel Stacey? She's agreed to take over Alec's coaching duties. So there's no thought of not going ahead with the game."

Archie threw back his head and brayed, "A woman coach! Har, har, har!"

"I have been a hockey coach for a number of years, Mr. Gillis," Muriel announced. "My team, the Charlottetown Cannonballs, have been five-time provincial champions. So I do know what I'm doing."

"Oh, I'm sure you do," sniggered Archie. "With women."

Muriel was unruffled. "A game is a game, Mr. Gillis, whether played by men or women."

"Well, we'll see about that on the ice!" challenged Archie, as he moved away.

"Oh dear, Muriel," fretted Hetty, "I hope whatever it is you have up your sleeve will stand us in good stead."

"Oh, it will, Hetty, it will," replied Muriel, trying to cover her own anxiety as, once again, she looked to see if anyone was coming down the road.

Abner Jeffries blew his whistle, the puck was dropped, a great cheer went up from the crowd and The Big Game was underway! The players bolted up and down the ice after the puck, which seemed to take on a life of its own, skidding and flying and spinning through the air. Felix huffed and puffed, trying to body-check Rupert Gillis, who always managed to be just beyond his reach at the critical moment. Rupert was just as determined to knock

Felix out of action and, halfway through the first half, cross-checked him right off the ice. As Felix sprawled in the snow, howling in pain because of a twisted wrist, Rupert scored a goal. The crowd roared as the Avengers took the lead!

Felix limped back to Muriel Stacey and Hetty, who were shouting instructions to the Misfits, now one man short.

"Sit down, Felix!" instructed Hetty, who by now was completely immersed in the game. "You've just had the wind knocked out of you. You'll be fine."

Felix wanted desperately to cry, but since it wasn't the "manly" thing to do, he choked back the tears.

"There, there, son," clucked Janet, "you just rest a bit, you'll get back in the game."

Sara looked at Felix, looked at the score and made her move.

"Miss Stacey, may I play now, please, please? I'm a sub and I've been practicing and we're one man short and—oh please, Miss Stacey?"

Muriel and Hetty exchanged looks, then nodded their agreement. Sara sprang onto the ice, to the cheers of the watching crowd.

"Felix," whispered Janet, as she rubbed her aching lower back, "I'm feeling a bit weary, so I think I'll go on up to the house now, all right, son?"

Felix was too distracted by his injuries to pay much notice as his mother walked away from the pond, taking deep breaths as she labored up to the house.

Remembering Peg's advice of Right Place and Right Time, Sara skated as best she could down the ice and positioned herself in front of the Avengers' net. The play whirled around her, up and down the rink, but Sara held her ground. She was absolutely determined to score a goal for the Misfits!

Finally, the opening came. Peg Bowen hurtled down the ice, deftly working the puck back and forth. She was brilliant! Amazing! And she was coming straight for Sara! Sara tensed, ready for the pass—this was her moment, the moment to tie the game, the moment to be in the Right Place at the Right Time, the moment to show the whole world that she was worth having on any team—ever! The puck left Peg Bowen's stick, arched gracefully through the air and landed right in front of Sara's stick. Sara turned, shot the puck straight toward the goal and—missed!

The crowd groaned—unbelievable! It was the best scoring opportunity the Misfits had had so far, and with only two minutes left to play in the first half things were not looking good. Sara was heartsick as she skated off the ice. It was true beyond a shadow of a doubt—she was a failure, plain and simple. Before this miserable effort she'd been ignored by her teammates; now she would be despised. And it wasn't just hockey, it was everything! Skating, helping Jasper with his goose, cows being born, making muffins—it was everything!

And Peg Bowen was just a big fake, with her Right Place at the Right Time nonsense!

Hetty's heart flooded with compassion as Sara wobbled towards her. Sara had tried so very hard, it seemed unfair to miss at the last moment. But life could be like that, thought Hetty. A split-second decision could change your entire future. Like the time she had turned down John MacIntyre's proposal of marriage. And now, as surely as Hetty was pierced by Sara's crestfallen look, she allowed herself to be pierced by the truth—the real truth—for the first time. Muriel Stacey hadn't stolen John away. No, no, that wasn't the way it had happened at all. The fact was, Hetty had let him go. All these years, she had gripped her prideful anger close, to shield herself against the pain. She had lost both a lover and her dearest friend because of that armor. Perhaps it was time to lay down her weapons and declare the peace. But first, poor Sara needed comforting.

"Sara, child," said Hetty, gently, as she gave Sara a rare hug, "you go on up to the house and get Aunt Janet to fix you some cocoa. You tried your best, Sara. That's all anyone can do. Don't be too hard on yourself, dear."

Sara turned away and trudged up to the house. If Felix didn't cry, darned if she would!

"Hetty, Hetty," cried Muriel, as Hetty watched Sara tramp away, "what are you day-dreaming about?

We've got a hockey game to win here! Now, who do you think we should send out as right wing?"

Alec King grimaced as he attempted to lift himself from the daybed in the kitchen, where he had been listening to the slap and roar of the hockey game in the distance. As Janet entered the house, Alec fell back, defeated. Between painful muscle spasms he choked out the one question on his mind.

"How—are the—Misfits doing?"

"Well, Alec," sighed Janet, sitting down heavily at the kitchen table, "the Avengers are leading one to nothing, so the Misfits are only losing by one goal. So far."

"Oh, Lord," mourned Alec, "I can't sit up. I can't lie down. I've never felt so helpless in all my life!"

Janet inhaled sharply. "Alec, I think it's time."

"Time for what, dear?"

Janet's eyes widened as the first real labor pain rippled through her body.

"The baby, Alec!" she gasped. "The baby!

Chapter Twelve

As Sara plodded towards the King farmhouse, she heard the whistle shrill back at the pond, signalling the end of the first half of the hockey game. All she wanted to do was throw herself into Aunt

Janet's understanding arms and sob away her disgrace. But what greeted Sara as she opened the kitchen door was a scene very different from what she had been imagining. Janet was sitting, leaning back on a kitchen chair, breathing deeply, holding her immense, alive belly. Her face was flushed and glistening as the effort of preparing to give birth showed its unmistakable effects. But it wasn't just effort and pain that played on Janet's features, it was something else—something wonderful and powerful—something deeply moving. A new life was about to enter the world! A little life about to breathe its first air, feel its first loving touch, nuzzle at its mother's breast! But first, Sara realized with alarm, it had to be born!

"Oh, Sara, thank goodness you're here!" panted Janet.

"Sara, run quickly and get Dr. Blair!" shouted Alec from his frozen position on the daybed. Sara spun towards the door, ready to race off.

"No!" shrieked Janet. "Don't go! Don't leave me alone!"

"You're not alone, dear," Alec called from across the room. "I'm here!"

Sara stopped at the door, confused. "What should I do!?"

"Oh, Alec, how can you help me?" gasped Janet. "You can't move!"

"I'll be fine, I'll be fine. Sara, quick, run!"

Sara broke into a cold sweat as she watched another deep contraction grip Janet's body, squeezing her breath into sharp bursts. This was definitely worse than when Sara had seen the calf being born!

"It's—too—late, Sara," gasped Janet. "Too—late!"

And it looked like it was too late for the Misfits, too, as they struggled onto the ice as the second half of the game got underway. It was becoming more and more clear that they were being outskated and overpowered by Archie Gillis and the mighty Avengers. The Misfits fans groaned in agony as the Avengers tallied up another goal, now making the score two to nothing.

"Well, Muriel," Hetty demanded, "where's the card up your sleeve? We're getting trounced and no two ways about it!"

Yet again, Muriel peered down the road and finally, *finally* saw what she had been anxiously watching for. Three sturdy young women, ruddy-cheeked and radiating strength, marched towards the King pond. They were uniformed in dark navy sweaters and skirts and each girl carried skates and well-worn hockey sticks. They looked magnificent, thought Muriel. They looked like victory!

"There you are, Hetty, there's my trump card! What you're seeing are the star players from the Charlottetown Cannonballs, come to join the fray."

Hetty's eyes shone as the young college women approached. "Oh, splendid, Muriel. Quite splendid indeed!" To Hetty's surprise, she was having quite a difficult time stopping herself from actually jumping up and down with excitement.

On the other side of the pond, Archie Gillis took stock of the situation. If the determined unison march of the women was any indication, the Avengers were in trouble.

"You mean they're gonna play, too?" he hollered across the ice. "It isn't fair. It's against the rules!"

"You told us to make up a team. And we have!" Muriel hurled back.

"Or are you afraid?" challenged Hetty.

"Afraid?" snorted Archie. "You're in a sorry state when you have to recruit more women!"

"See you on the ice, Archie," retorted Peg Bowen, as the crowd picked up the chant "Misfits! Misfits! Misfits—Go!!"

Sara tripped down the stairs to get a cool cloth to soothe Janet's perspiring forehead. Alec lay helplessly on the daybed, unable to do anything other than worry.

"How are things going, Sara?" he asked, anxiously,

"Oh, fine—I think—oh, I don't know! Aunt Janet says everything is proceeding according to normal, but I've never seen a baby born before so—"

Felicity burst through the door. "We just tied the game!" she blared, as she danced around the kitchen.

"Ellie Martin, one of the Cannonballs, scored a goal right away! And then another one! The score's tied two-all! Oh, you should have seen Archie Gillis's face, you should have!!"

"Felicity, there's something much more important happening than the game," interrupted Sara, "and I need your help—right now!"

Felicity's excited state deafened her to Sara's news, and she continued to hop up and down.

"We're going to win!" Felicity shouted. "Win! Win! Win!!"

"Felicity!" roared Alec. Then, more quietly, "Your mother's having the baby."

Felicity stopped. Her mouth flew open. "Wha-wha-what?"

Sara nodded. "She's upstairs in bed. I've made her as comfortable as I can but thank goodness you're here, Felicity. You know a lot more about babies than I do, so you can take care of things from here on in. I'll run and fetch Dr. Blair."

Felicity's response was to turn white, roll her eyes back and drop to the floor in a dead faint.

"Oh, no!" chorused Sara and Alec. "Felicity, how could you?" squawked Sara.

A passionate cry from Janet ricocheted down the stairs. "Sara! Alec! Come quickly!"

Sara stepped over Felicity and sprinted towards the hall. "Excuse me, Uncle Alec. I think I'm needed elsewhere."

Upstairs, Janet lay on the bed, breathing heavily with a deep contraction that pushed the almost-born baby closer and closer to its final destination. Sara gripped Janet's hand. It was a strange thing, thought Sara, but she was beginning to feel calmer as the actual birth approached. She had the feeling that something wonderful and natural was happening, and she wasn't disgusted or frightened at all—in fact, she was getting excited!

"Aunt Janet, what do you want me to do? What can I do?"

As the contraction passed, Janet breathed more regularly once again. "Just stay with me, Sara, I'll tell you what to do."

"But you're in pain!" cried Sara.

Janet smiled. "I know, dear. But it's natural. It's normal. How's poor Alec?"

As Sara was about to reply, an ashen-faced Felicity appeared at the door. She swayed slightly, in ghostly fashion, as her glazed eyes took in the scene.

"Oh, Felicity!" exclaimed Sara. "You know more about this than I do. What happens next? What do we do?"

But all Sara's questions went unanswered as Felicity fell once again into a swoon.

"Felicity! Don't!" commanded Sara, but Felicity was past hearing her as she slowly crumpled to a heap.

Janet gripped Sara's hand with amazing strength as a final, massive contraction seized her body.

"Oh, here it is, Sara! Here—oh, my Lord—ooohhhh—"

And then, as Sara watched in amazement and wonder, the tiniest King entered the world, guided by Sara's trembling hands. Sara could hardly speak, she was so overwhelmed.

"I think—it's a boy, Aunt Janet!" she croaked.

Janet sobbed with exhaustion and relief as Sara hugged her close. "Sara, Sara—thank you." And the two hugged each other and wept together.

Then, as the infant boy instinctively howled his greeting to humanity, Janet instructed Sara as to what to do. Sara washed the wee fellow, wrapped him in a cozy flannel blanket, kissed his dewy head and handed him to Janet. When the baby was nestled safely in Janet's loving arms, she smiled a radiant, weary smile.

"You see, Sara, you dear, shining girl, you're not a failure at all! When I needed you most, you were at my side. Your mother and father would be so proud of you, Sara, and make no mistake—you *are* part of our family." Then Janet, exhausted, closed her eyes.

Sara found herself trembling with excitement and emotion. "Oh, thank you, Aunt Janet," she whispered, "thank you."

"Misfits! Misfits! Misfits!" chanted the crowd as the final minutes of the hockey game built to a frenzy.

"Avengers! Avengers! Avengers!" bellowed fans on the opposite side, rooting their team to victory.

Muriel and Hetty shouted encouragement to the Misfits as they skated desperately to score the tie-breaking, game-winning goal. Up and down the ice they raced, passing, firing, checking—but always intercepted by the Avengers. Abner Jeffries checked his stopwatch—thirty seconds to go!

Andrew King passed to Felix, but the pass was blocked by Malcolm MacGinty, who fired the puck to Rupert, who streaked towards the Misfits goal! Rupert shot towards the net—he missed!

The crowd roared as Peg Bowen dug the puck out of the corner and raced toward the Avengers goal, passing the puck to Ellie Martin halfway down the ice. Ellie sprinted forward as Peg skated backwards with incredible speed. Peg whirled in front of the Avengers' goal, waiting for Ellie's pass. It came—a perfect pass that somehow magically threaded its way through a forest of Avengers! Peg spun round, set her stick and shot the puck towards the goal—a beautiful shot! It lifted, whirled and sizzled past the goalie! The crowd went wild! The whistle blew! Final score—Misfits-3, Avengers-2!

Hetty and Muriel hugged each other, jumping up and down with jubilation as the Misfits circled the ice, victorious, their hockey sticks held high.

Peg Bowen stopped in front of Archie Gillis.

Archie extended his hand. "You won fair and square, Peg Bowen. I hate to admit it, but you did."

Peg didn't take his hand. Not yet. "I hope you remember our bargain, Archie."

"I'm not a man to go back on my word," Archie assured her. "I won't touch the trees anywhere near your cabin or in the town of Avonlea. You have my promise."

Peg shook Archie's hand, resolutely. "And, for my part, I hereby lift the curse on your hockey team."

"There wasn't a curse," said Archie, "was there?"

Peg laughed wickedly as she skated away, leaving Archie Gillis to forever ponder the possibility.

And so it was that everyone crowded into the King farmhouse for a victory celebration, only to discover that, once again, the miracle of birth had visited Avonlea. Felix fetched Dr. Blair, who declared both mother and child and the twice-fainted Felicity completely well. He also congratulated Sara on her steadfast assistance and "presence of mind."

"Holy Dinah," Felix kept saying to Cecily, "we've got a baby brother!" And Cecily Holy Dinah'd right back.

Glasses of Janet's raspberry cordial were lifted in toasts to the new mother, to the new baby, to Alec, to Sara, to the victorious Misfits and, finally, to life itself, in all its amazing varieties and forms.

"And you see, Sara," whispered Peg Bowen on her way out the door at the end of the celebrations, "you were in the Right Place at the Right Time, after all."

Sara could only nod her agreement as she stared into Peg's dark, wise eyes.

The fire crackled and jumped in the parlor fireplace of Rose Cottage, casting a cheerful glow on Hetty, Muriel and Sara. Olivia had gone up to her room, to work on her article for the *Chronicle*. "So much to tell!" she had exclaimed, as she gathered up her notes and bade the others good night.

What a day it had been! thought Sara. What an adventure!

Hetty poured Muriel another cup of thick cocoa. Then she straightened up and cleared her throat.

"Muriel, I—well, there's something I would like to say to you."

Muriel nodded. "Of course, Hetty. I knew you'd honor our bargain, and I'm sure you'll find intramural sports in the Avonlea curriculum quite exciting. You know, Hetty, I think you've got a flair for coaching, I really do."

"Thank you, perhaps, but—it's a rather more personal matter I want to discuss with you," replied Hetty.

"I suppose you want me to leave," sighed Sara.

"Not at all," said Hetty. "As a matter of fact, I would like you to hear this." Hetty took a deep breath. "Muriel, I owe you an apology. One that's twenty years overdue. Please, please don't say anything—just let me speak. The truth is, you see, that I truly did love John MacIntyre, but I was afraid of that passion. Of course I was young, and that's what my parents kept saying. They insisted that I come back to Avonlea for a couple of years, but, I have to face it—I let them insist. And a couple of years turned into several years, and, finally, John gave up. He melted away, like a forgotten snowman in a warm, winter sun. And I've always known, Muriel, deep in my heart, that it wasn't until then that you and John got engaged. You didn't steal him from me. I let him go. And I've wronged you all these years. I'm so very sorry, Muriel—so very sorry."

Sara had never seen Hetty so vulnerable, so open. So that's what love could do to you—soften your soul, open your heart, ease the pain of living. Sara could almost glimpse the young woman Hetty had been, peeking out from the often stern, middle-aged face.

"What did happen between you and John, Miss Stacey?" asked Sara, somehow knowing that it was a question waiting to be asked.

Muriel spoke simply, and her rich voice warmed the room.

"We were lonely, and we thought we might make a go of it. But I think we always knew that we weren't really in love with each other. You see, Sara, I don't think John ever got over Hetty—not really. Oh, he eventually married someone else, but I always remember him saying to me 'There's only one Hetty.'"

And that was the end of the story. A gentle silence drifted down on the parlor, and Sara found herself overtaken by an immense yawn. After she said her good nights and went up to bed, Hetty and Muriel stayed in the parlor, gazing at the fire. Once again, they were two friends sitting side by side, sharing memories and, if all went well, sharing thoughts of the future, too.

As Sara lay in the soft dark of her room, she could hear their voices gently rising and falling like the ocean, like the soft breathing of the miraculous newborn nestled in Janet's arms, like Peg Bowen's coal-black eyes, like the bittersweet memory of her mother and father, like the ebb and flow of life itself. And Sara understood that life wasn't a matter of winning and losing, succeeding or failing. Life was a matter of being ready, open and willing—always willing—to be surprised by love. That was the real miracle.

Sara smiled into the dark. "We're misfits all," she thought, as she drifted into a deep, healing sleep.

Outside, the Northern Lights rippled silently back and forth across the winter sky above Avonlea—dancing, sweeping reds and greens—magical, eternal.

❦   ❦   ❦